The Wrong Twin Dilemma

Hayden Hall

THE

DILEMMA

HAYDEN HALL

About the Book

He's as off-limits as a guy can be. So why do I want no one but him?
London
Of all the guys in the world, I just had to fall hopelessly and irreparably in love with my twin sister's boyfriend. No amount of parties with happy endings can put him out of my mind.
Gabriel is also a dork, but he's a hot as all hell dork. Somehow, he's both a nerd and a jock and he pushes all my buttons. But he's straight. He shouldn't attract me the way he does. And did I mention they've been dating for two years? Yeah... They're all but married.
I'm officially the worst brother – and human, let's not pretend – in the history of ever.
And when my genius of a sister comes up with a bulletproof plan to help me pass my exams by convincing Gabriel to tutor me, I discover that my big, beautiful dork hides a secret even more ruinous than my own. The way he looks at me

when we're alone is almost all I've ever dreamed
of.
But how many hearts will shatter if I take what I
want? Is it not better that I let my love die quietly?
I hate wanting him.

Gabriel

I'm a hot mess and he's off limits. We are a disaster
in the making.
I can't say no to tutoring London. It would look like
I'm hiding something, which I'm *totally not*. But if
I were hiding something, it would not be easy to
keep it hidden once the lessons begin and we're
alone.
He crawls under my skin before I know it. He fills
my mind with his rosy lips, high cheekbones, and
sculped muscles. His *male* muscles, which I *totally
don't like*. Except, when I'm alone, letting him into
my thoughts is a comfort I desperately need.
The more I'm with him, the more I see I might
be dating the wrong twin. But there's no easy way
out of it. There's no happy ending for anyone here.
Unless...
Unless I do what I fear the most and own up to the
truth: *London is all I ever wanted.*

*The Wrong Twin Dilemma is the third book in the Frat
Brats of Santa Barbara series. It features one dorky,
straight jock, one player with a bruised and tender heart,
a whole lot of pining, a journey of discovering new sensations (wink, wink), and a grand finale to resolve the
mess they make. There is NO CHEATING of any sort
and there is a happy ending for EVERYONE involved.
The book can be read on its own, but it's just more fun to
start with The Fake Boyfriends Debacle.*

Contents

CHAPTER ONE

London and Elle

THE SWORD NEARLY CHOPPED my head off.

"Bro!" Andy grabbed fistfuls of his shaggy hair and gaped. "How did you...?"

"You don't get this skill overnight," I said, evading the monstrosity that was standing between me and the Midnight Fractal.

"Holy fuck, Gabriel," Andy whispered.

"Wait, wait," I said, my thumbs aching like hell at this point. I made a few risky moves, maneuvered around the Soulless that was protecting the prize, and unleashed hell upon my joystick. "This..." The epic music kicked in, blasting out of our surround system — courtesy of my father — and Andy all but peed his freaking pants.

To be fair, the hairs on my neck rose. Were I not in the most epic boss-fight of the game, I would take a moment to appreciate the sounds of a full orchestra.

"You know they recorded all the music at *Abbey Road Studios*?" I asked. Game trivia was one of my richest areas of knowledge. It was right next to high-level economics and gym exercises. If there were gaps in my knowledge, they weren't in any of these three.

Andy — whose mouth had been hanging open — dislodged his jaw in awe. "You're shitting me."

"Nope. Every note of the entire game was recorded there," I said as I ran to hide behind a conveniently placed boulder. The Soulless would soon come looking and its legs would be exposed. "There you are," I sneered at the monster and jumped out from behind the boulder. My abs literally tensed; hell, all my muscles tensed as I swung my saber at the beast's legs. Once, twice, thrice, and the damage was done. It couldn't move as fast any longer and that was all the advantage I needed to beat it.

"You're actually going to do it," Andy said. "Motherfucker, you're actually going to do it!"

"Just you wait," I said with a note of pride. Not only was I going to win the boss-fight, but I was going to win it on my first try.

A minute before I could have ended the fight, my phone lit up and buzzed between my legs, tangled in the blanket. I hit *pause* as soon as I saw Elle's photo glowing on my screen and picked up.

"Hey babe. What's up?" I asked and virtually threw myself back onto the bed, head sinking into the pillow.

"Are you kidding me?" Andy growled.

I waved at him to be quiet.

Obeying, he whispered, "Not everyone likes being edged, Gabriel."

"Not much," Elle said. "I just got out of the last lecture. Are you up to anything good?"

"Does edging Andy count?" I joked. Andy rolled his eyes and Elle screamed with laughter. "I'm showing him *The Seeds of Soulless.*"

"Ah, flexing," she said. "Are we set for tonight?"

"You bet we are," I said. "I have to run to the library before I can meet you. Seven's alright?"

"Perfect," she said. "Love you."

"Love you too," I said just as she hung up. I couldn't help but feel it had become a little too mechanical to end a conversation that way. But we'd said that to one another a year earlier for the first time when it truly felt special. Not that we didn't love each other. We did. It just felt a little too effortless on both sides.

Loving someone was one thing. Saying it out of a habit was vastly different. In my opinion, at least.

"*Wove you,*" Andy mocked.

I wagged my index finger at him. "And for that, my friend, you don't get to metaphorically come today."

It looked like he was fighting between rolling his eyes and widening them in despair. "Come on, you're like five minutes away from finishing it off."

"If my father could hear this out of context," I mused. We'd made plenty of innuendos that would probably make my father's face turn royally purple. "But I have to run. We can play tomorrow."

Andy grumbled and shook his head at me as he picked up the joystick and saved my progress.

As I got up, my muscles burned. I'd overworked myself in the gym the day before and now I paid the price. But it was a nice, searing feeling of progress, so I didn't complain much.

It's not like I'd have any physical activity tonight-, I thought, then frowned at the bitter taste the thought had left in my mouth. I hated being like this. Resentment was not what I was about. But sometimes — rarely, to be fair — it seeped through. Elle and I hadn't had the most passionate behind-the-doors relationship and that was fine. It was alright. We didn't have to have sex all the time. But still, once in a while, resentment would fill me to the brink of despair and a nasty thought would make itself comfortable in my mind. Weren't we supposed to be crazy about each other at this age? Weren't we supposed to use every chance we got? Instead, we'd done it a few times, early on, and never, ever again. I had a hard time instigating it; she had a hard time getting into the mood. Sometimes, it was the other way around. Either way, it just didn't happen. And most of the time, I kept reminding myself that it's not about sex... *But...*

I picked up my phone, keys, and backpack. My first stop was the library. The first week of the new semester had caught me off guard. The curriculum was a tad more challenging than in the first and second years, but if I wasn't a fan of a good challenge, nobody was.

The afternoon air was slightly breezy, bringing a bit of relief from the heatwave that had kept us all on the beach for weeks and weeks. Or, just as often, holed up in air-conditioned rooms with *Seeds of Soulless* as the finest form of entertainment. Yeah, I liked my games.

I walked into the library on campus and made my steady way to the economics section. My dinner with Elle loomed large over my head. Not that I had anything in particular to worry about. It was just that, lately, we hadn't really seen eye to eye. I loved her to death and had no doubt that the feeling was mutual, but two years in, we were starting to get bored. Spicing things up with hobbies, as much as in the bedroom, didn't seem to do the trick.

For a moment, I was tempted to seek a self-help section in the library, but I quickly pushed that thought away. I was on a mission here. I needed my extra literature to catch up on everything before the semester ran me over.

Juggling a social life, personal interests, studies, and fitness was starting to become a bit of a problem. Adding a relationship that kept taking a backseat in both our lives was just a little too much. But after two years, there was no way I was just going to give up.

We needed something special. Or... *I'm not thinking about that*. But I still wondered what it was all for.

A grunt from the other side of the bookcase pulled me out of my thoughts. I recognized that voice. I'd grown up near that voice. Just like Elle and I had been close since we could walk, this voice was always there, orbiting us, sometimes up close, sometimes from afar.

I walked to the edge of the bookcase and poked my head around to the other side. A wiry and fit, light brunette guy with delicate fingers and muscled arms sighed in frustration. It was Elle's twin brother — or, her younger brother, as she liked to point out, because he came into the world a couple of minutes after her — and he wasn't having fun here.

"Need a hand?" I asked.

London Reynolds's furious gaze met my eyes and he softened. "Agh... No. I'm good."

"Sure you are. Nothing like a good growl to celebrate finding the right book." I grinned at him.

In return, London fidgeted around and scratched the back of his head awkwardly. "It's not a big deal."

I nodded. "I'll leave you to your growling, then."

As I pulled back, London made a panicked half-step toward me. "Wait."

I straightened and walked up to him, leaned against the bookcase, and raised my eyebrows to match my smile.

London's cheeks were rosy and his big, brown eyes warm. He rarely looked right into my eyes. And when he did, it didn't last long. We'd never really been close friends, though we'd known each other our entire lives. Sure, we would hang out, the three of us, every once in a while, but London and I had never been alone in the same place. Not that it mattered.

He cleared his throat and met my curious gaze. "I'm taking Managerial Economics again."

"What made you do that?" I teased.

He scoffed. "Just doing it for the joy of it."

"Right." I scanned around the bookcases. "And you need...?"

He rubbed the temples on his head, then moved a messy lock of light brunette hair from his right eye. He had a gentle way of doing this, just like Elle. It reminded me of her so much that I almost pointed it out, but stopped myself. I knew, for sure, that Elle wasn't a huge fan of people pointing out their similarities. And I could sort of understand that. They shared everything, from the color of their hair, to their eyes, to their sharp cheekbones and perfect little noses. The rest of us walked around all unique and only-one-like-this-in-existence style, while they had to put up with the fact there was an exact replica of them.

They loved each other beyond belief and could almost read each other's thoughts, though. I never saw any resentment in them, but they made it clear they wanted to be their own people.

"So I flunked because I didn't understand a word of the textbook. It's kinda funny that our very own professor wrote it, but never mind. I was hoping I'd find something like...a guide for dummies." He rolled his eyes. It was like he was pulling his own tooth, rather than saying this.

"First of all, you're not a dummy," I said.

He cut in. "Spare me the affirmation. That's not why I'm here."

I snorted. "I know just the book you need," I said.

"Yeah?" He actually lit up a little.

"But I won't tell you."

His frown and bobbing of the head indicated a mixture of surprise and proper Reynolds annoyance. I knew this gesture, too, from Elle.

I laughed. "I won't tell you until you say 'I am not a dummy.'"

London rolled his eyes, but at me, this time. "Ever thought of being a motivational speaker? You'd make a killing."

I shrugged. "I don't need a killing."

"Daddy's got you covered," he joked.

"And yours doesn't?" I teased back.

"Touché, my friend." He took a deep breath of air, sighed, then inhaled again. "I am not a dummy."

"See? That wasn't so hard after all." I crossed my arms at my chest.

"And I feel a gazillion times better. Thank you, Sensei." Sarcasm dripped from his voice so much there was an actual puddle of it on the floor between us.

Laughter spurted out of me before I could stop myself. I was pretty damn sure I heard several shushes from around the library, so I sealed my lips and fought my laughter back inside.

Shaking my head, I walked to the far end of the bookcase and scanned the spines of various books.

"I don't even understand the titles of any of those," London said with all the despair of a self-defeatist that he was.

"*I am not a dummy*," I chanted and pulled out a small paperback with a plain blue spine and thickly printed words, *Lead With Confidence*. I handed it to London. "You should be able to understand this much."

London's eyes narrowed. "Seriously? Some self-help crap?"

I laughed again, but cut it short. "Trust me. It's not what it sounds like. Just give it a read. It'll introduce you to the most basic principles of good leadership, backed by internal and external company economics. At the very least, you'll know which questions to ask yourself and what to read next."

Suspecting of it, London flipped through the book. He snorted. "There aren't even any photos." The corners of his lips twitched briefly as he suppressed a smile. His gaze met mine and he seemed...different. "Thanks."

"No problem," I said. "And when you're done, let me know. I'll tell you what you need to read next."

He raised one neatly manicured, black eyebrow. "Is it gonna help me pass Managerial or are we just gonna have some more things to talk about?"

I couldn't help myself but laugh. "Both. Trust me and you'll pass with flying colors."

"I don't need flying colors," he said. "Hell, they'll just suspect me of cheating if I score above the passing grade."

I winked at him and tapped the book he was holding. "Just do what I say."

The pinkness in his cheeks seemed to intensify, but I didn't have enough time to think about its meaning. London raised a hand to the back of his head, the short sleeve sliding up his biceps. He was at least thirty pounds lighter than me and a good five inches shorter. Still, he was pretty tall, and I was the six-foot-six, two-hundred-pound gym-freak. But London was a first class swimmer and a casual gym goer, so his biceps naturally flexed as he bent his arm. The sculpted muscle rose and I caught the faint hint of a vein, much more prominent in his forearm. His creamy skin was smooth and looked soft. It looked as soft as Elle's, but taut over the bulge of the muscle.

I took a quick breath of air and blinked, then looked away. My stomach felt light, but my chest felt heavy. "I gotta bounce, man," I said, my voice a husky whisper.

As I passed him, he scratched his head a little more, running his slim fingers through his rich, light brunette hair. "Thanks again."

"Yeah," I said, breathless, as I turned around the bookcase and left the library. It was only when I was halfway across campus that I remembered I hadn't picked up any of the books I needed. But time was running away from me and Elle didn't like tardiness. I didn't like it, either. 'He was punctual,' wouldn't be a wrong epitaph for my tombstone, someday.

The sun was beginning to kiss the horizon by the time I reached the bistro bar. Elle got there just a minute after I neared the table I'd booked earlier. I got up and hugged her. "Missed you today," I said. "Hell, I've missed you this whole week."

We'd been on vacation together during the final two weeks of summer break, but I'd barely seen her since.

"Missed you too," she said and pecked me on the cheek. Yeah, it wasn't like I was dying to make out in public, but I couldn't hold back a mischievous smile at the innocence of that kiss.

Elle didn't seem to notice. She sat down across from me and let her head fall back. She closed her eyes and took a moment to bathe in the flaming orange glow of the setting sun. The terrace of the bar was supported by iron beams on which the wooden floor rested. The ocean's waves crashed into the rocks beneath the deck and if I chose a distant point to look at, it almost seemed like the entire bistro was floating.

"I saw London just now," I said.

"Mm." Elle soaked up all the sunshine she could get. "Out on a date?"

I chuckled. It wouldn't have surprised me. "Actually, no. I saw him at the library."

Elle's head shot up and she laughed. "Is he ill? What the hell?"

"He looked miserable, poor thing. Managerial is kicking his ass." I glanced at the menu, but it was a force of habit. I was the kind of guy who had a *usual* and went for it.

Elle growled. "Managerial."

"You passed it," I pointed out.

She smiled. Her smile was so much like London's it was crazy. "I passed it, but I almost failed every other course."

I rolled my eyes playfully. "You aced them all, Elle."

She drew on an air of pride. "I'm awesome." She followed it with a chuckle. "So, my little bro is actually trying to study this year."

"He's trying to," I said. Managerial Economics wasn't so hard on me, but I'd spent the summer leading up to my enrollment reading up on everything that lay ahead. It was a legitimately hard course and very, *very* mandatory.

Elle frowned. "You gave him *Leading With Confidence*, didn't you?"

I laughed. "You bet I did."

Her eyes narrowed as a plan unfolded somewhere inside her head. She tapped her chin with her index finger and leaned in. "Babe, would you maybe tutor him?"

I snort-chuckled. It was a ridiculous idea. London Reynolds did not like being taught lessons by his professors, let alone a college junior who dated his sister. Besides, thinking of being around him by myself made that odd feeling return. My stomach was hollow as soon as I pictured sitting next to him and pointing at the page in a book. He'd be too close. He'd be too short-sleeved and head-scratchy. He'd be too...London. "Like he'd ever accept that," I said.

"It's not up to him. There's no way he'll pass that exam without help." She raised one neat, black eyebrow exactly the way London had. "He could really use some help."

I rubbed the back of my neck and looked away from her. I wanted to help him. But I wasn't so sure about whatever this feeling inside of me was. *Pull yourself together, man*, I hissed at myself internally. *You're imagining things*.

Thoughtlessly, I began to nod. "I guess I could." Chills passed down my spine. "I mean, it won't harm him, but I'll bet he won't be thrilled. He almost barked at me when I offered to help him with a book."

Elle laughed. "That's London. You can't do him a favor without making it look like he's doing you a favor, instead."

I chuckled. Elle was like that, too. "Fine, I guess. I can help a bro out."

Her smile was very sweet after that. She'd always been the one uniting the three of us. Even though we'd orbited each other since we were kids, Elle was always in between. She was the one to organize movie nights and going out, she was the one that had me and London sitting on either side of her. She was the one who wanted to keep that childhood bond alive, even if there had never really been a bond there between London and me.

We ordered our food and drinks, caught up on the events of the week, threw around some ideas for what to do in the coming months, and that was pretty much our date. Nothing of any importance had actually happened in the past five days to either of us. Nothing out of the ordinary. Well, except that thing that twisted my lungs earlier today, but *that* wasn't noteworthy.

After another round of drinks, we decided to take a walk by the beach. It was already dark outside and the ocean breeze brought us some much-needed relief. It also pushed a lock of Elle's hair over her left eye and she raised her hand to her face. The slender fingers removed the lock and an image of London doing the same thing raised my pulse.

I ignored it.

"I forgot to tell you," she said. "My parents are throwing a fundraiser in six weeks. It's actually very elaborate with a gala one evening, an auction the next, and a series of guest performances by some of the really popular artists in California."

"That sounds interesting," I said. My mind was elsewhere, though I didn't want it there.

"They'd like us to be present," she said. "Something about young faces and all that."

I chuckled. "We can show up and be pretty."

"Should I confirm it, then?" she asked.

"Sure," I said.

She took her phone out immediately and tapped at her screen for a few moments. My phone buzzed with an update to my calendar, blocking an extended weekend for this event.

"Perfect," Elle said. A moment later, she yawned and tightened her hand around my elbow. "I think I'll head back, babe."

I nodded. "Me too. Andy's gonna disown me if I don't finish our boss-fight tonight."

Elle chuckled. She was the only girl I knew who seriously enjoyed a good video game. She rarely played them, but she could appreciate them as well as a hardened gamer like myself.

We faced each other and she lifted her chin for a goodbye kiss.

I put one hand on her smooth cheek and leaned in. My lips pressed against hers and an inexplicable sadness overwhelmed me. It felt as though neither of us really wanted this. It felt as though we loved each other much more when we loved from afar.

Trying to suppress this feeling, I parted my lips further and dialed up the passion. Darkness filled my blank mind and sparks swirled around it, out of nowhere. It was all I could do not to pull back in a fright. The image that crossed my mind — a silly, ridiculous, twisted image — tugged me away from Elle, but I persisted. I kept the kiss going despite every cell in my body screaming to stop. In front of my closed eyes, it wasn't Elle's face.

Though it looked almost the same.

When Elle moved her head back, I caught a breath of air and forced a smile on. My insides turned and I pecked her cheek, then touched her shoulder. "Love you, babe."

"Love you, too," she said.

And with that, she walked away.

I stayed on the beach for a while longer as my heart pounded in my throat. I couldn't swallow. I couldn't move. That had not been okay. I was kissing my girlfriend of two years, but the sparks came on when I thought of her brother.

I was going to be sick.

Slowly, I lowered myself. My legs crossed under my ass and I sat with my head in my hands, elbows resting on my knees. *Holy shit. Holy shit. Holy shit. This isn't happening.*

My breathing returned to normal because I forced it to. Otherwise, it would have gone on just as quickly. These shallow breaths wouldn't keep me alive and conscious.

Why the fuck would I think of London?

Holy shit.

My heart kept racing, every other beat dropping somewhere empty, somewhere nonexistent. Sweat broke out under my arms and I took a deep breath of air, then held it. It had just been a thought. A trick of my mind. It didn't mean anything.

I'd seen London, I'd mentioned London, I was about to tutor London. He was on my mind for no other reason. None at all.

Yet my cock had gotten hard and my stomach had sparked with a million fluttering butterflies while I kissed Elle.

You kissed Elle, dude, my voice of reason tried telling me. *You got hard because you kissed Elle. Mystery solved.*

I gave a jerky nod, then quickly lifted my head to see if anyone saw me do it. I was all alone. I had no reason to nod at anything at all. And I was fine.

I was totally, totally fine.

CHAPTER TWO

A Study Buddy

———ele———

"IS HE CROWNING YET?" I barged into the room to an uproar of laughter. It was a terrible joke. Joshua wasn't even up for a crown, but I couldn't resist taking a stab right from the get go. All brotherly love, of course.

"Ha-ha, asshole," said Joshua from the tablet screen. "Nice job being punctual."

Dayton, comfortable in his armchair, snorted. "It's what I call a London timezone."

Passing by him, I punched his shoulder lightly. He slapped the place I'd touched and howled, feigning a fallen soldier type. "Shut it," I scoffed. "You're beating Caleb at the acting game."

"Where *is* Mr. Hamlet, anyway?" Joshua asked.

I looked around the dark red and brown common room at the ground floor of our dormitory, lit by the orange glow of the many small lamps, and shrugged. "Not here. Net yet, anyway."

"Congratulations. You're not the worst friend I have," Joshua said. "Screw it. I'm opening this beer."

"I thought you'd be drinking chardonnay made by the blind nuns from the Iberian hills, Your Majesty," I teased. I'd rarely had a chance to tease him since he'd taken off with Mateo, an actual, real life prince.

"Treason!" Joshua called and everyone in the room erupted in laughter. "Guards! Seize this fuckboy."

I ran a hand over my face, removing a persistent lock of hair that covered my right eye. Stefan and Marco distributed the cold ones for everyone in the room. I cracked mine open and took a long sip after the shitshow of a day I'd had.

"I'll have you know, if you ever mean to visit the Royal Palace, you'll need to know the etiquette. His Majesty is only used when speaking of the King, Queen, and the King Regent." Joshua took a sip of his beer and gave a satisfying 'ah.' I fucking missed him.

We did these group calls once every blue moon. I got it; he was busy. We were all busy, but Joshua especially. He was learning Spanish when he wasn't studying history or smooching with his prince. And I was happy for him. At least some of us found happiness.

The last time I'd seen him in person was a few months earlier. Caleb had finally premiered as Hamlet, but first, he'd made Joshua swear he would find a way to visit if he scored the role. Unbeknownst to Joshua, Caleb had already had the role, but the trick worked and we got to spend some time with our favorite royal.

"So what do I call you?" I asked in the middle of a euphoric clamor in the large room. "Jester?"

"Joshua will suffice. For now," he said sneakily and his eyes shone.

"Please don't tell us you're getting married," I joked. "Dayton, he's getting married."

Joshua cackled. "I am not getting married." He gave a little shrug. "Yet, at least." But he followed that with another laugh. "How's life in Santa Barbara?"

I really didn't want to answer that question. Luckily for me, eight of our other friends jumped at the opportunity to tell Joshua everything that was going on since his last visit.

My life in Santa Barbara was a hot mess. Managerial Economics that I had failed was still haunting me and I didn't even want to come close to discussing my relationship status. I was still a certified bachelor who got the mileage from every hookup app under the gay sun. It wasn't something to brag about, but it did the trick. Every few days, I would hit it off with someone who could distract me for a night; someone who needed a distraction just as badly.

The entrance door of our common room flew open and in strolled Caleb with his arm thrown over Jayden. The two lovebirds were doe-eyed for one another to the point where the corners of my lips curled up and I had to force my smile away.

Maybe I was a softy for a sweet love story — maybe I had a pile of romance novels that nobody knew about under my bed — but I would rather die than let the others know. Especially when my own love story seemed to have been written by a Russian realist. Maybe I was just a character in a Dosto-evsky-style depression fest. I could totally picture it; the boring, slowly unraveling tale of betrayal, copious amounts of alcohol, and an early grave, but with a bunch of meaningless sex along the way.

A bunch of sex? Maybe I didn't have it that bad after all.

Caleb walked up to Joshua and kissed the damn tablet and everybody more or less pissed them-selves. "Looks like everyone here is early," Caleb said.

"Yes, the world is crazy, but you are sane," Joshua said.

Jayden shrugged. "You were almost late to his play."

"That room is full of traitors, I swear," Joshua proclaimed.

Caleb and Jayden crashed on the sofa that com-fortably seated three people. It was lucky for me because I was the third. It was sort of appropriate. I was everybody's third wheel. Caleb had Jayden; Joshua had Mateo; Elle had Gabriel.

I glanced around the room. Stefan had Mar-co. But that wasn't spoken aloud. Everyone knew those two touched each other's naked bits in the summer camp a little more than a year ago, but we pretended we didn't. And every single one of the guys in this room always had some nice guy under their arms, just like I did.

At times, I wondered if I was supposed to fall in love with one of my friends. That would have been easier for sure. We already got along and knew each other. But I was *not* attracted to any single one of them. And luckily for everyone involved, none of them were attracted to me, either.

No; my unrequited love lay elsewhere.

We dicked around for a couple of hours, Caleb taking the spotlight for most of that time. After all, the two of them had practically been conjoined since they were born. And a couple of beers later, the party thinned. My friends, and fraternity brothers by tradition, headed out one by one, probably hooking up. It was Friday; I was supposed to go out with them. I was supposed to drown my sorrows in seducing a hottie and, just maybe, eating said hottie's ass.

Tonight, though, I passed.

After Joshua left, Caleb and Jayden lingered around a little longer. Jayden, predictably, had three different international projects to juggle, so he called it a night for the three of us. It was a relief, to be honest. I couldn't force myself to stay cheerful this late at night and I would rather die than tell them the reason behind my grim face.

This was the second year of our studies. This was the second year of us all officially being free. I was supposed to be happy by now, but my grimness only ever went deeper.

After I saw Caleb and Jayden out, I found my backpack and took out the book Gabriel had given me. It was stupid, but I stared at the front cover of the book like it was Gabriel's photo. I was pathetic. And treacherous so long as I allowed myself to think about him like this. The guy was practically married to my sister.

So why did he have to be so fucking hot? Why did Elle and I have to have the same type? Why did we have to be so alike that we would both fall for the dorky, muscled, game-nerd, sexy...*stop that*, I internally shouted.

At last, I crashed into one of the armchairs, threw a leg over the arm holder, and opened the book. My heart trembled and my brain assassinated my goals for the night by reminding me that the last person who had touched this book was Gabriel. The cute, handsome Gabriel.

I rolled my eyes at myself and forced my brain to focus. Once the words started sinking in, I completely lost myself in *Lead With Confidence*. It was not even close to what I had expected. I had thought it would be a book filled with quasi-science of non-verbal communication in business meetings. Instead, I was reading accounts of world-changing decisions based on careful reviews of economics within the companies. By the time I gave an exhausted yawn, I was already halfway through the book and my head was filled with more questions.

He had been right. I knew where I needed to start.

Hell, it would not be easy. Managerial Economics was a notorious subject, often used to separate the students who would make it, from those who had never been meant to graduate from Highgate. But just now, I felt ever so slightly better about my chances. And if I were lucky, I would run into

Gabriel at the library and he would tell me what to do next.

I dragged my ass to the dorm room where Hudson's bed was empty and neat. The fucker was out there, having fun. Nothing in this world could bring his spirit down. I was pretty sure that the world would be ending and Hudson would still have a date lined up.

All I could do was say a silent prayer that he wouldn't bring his date over. The late-night text alerts to vacate the room were rare enough, but they happened. And, in fairness, he did the same for me, but it didn't make the instances any less annoying.

As I lay in my bed, my thoughts drifted back to Gabriel. I picked up my phone and opened an Instagram page, then scrolled through it. I'd done it a million times. I'd done it before going to bed nearly every night for the last four years, maybe longer. It wasn't even curiosity that compelled me to do it. There was nothing new on his page that I'd missed. And it wasn't for the lack of seeing his face, either. I'd seen him every week since I could remember. Perhaps the only thing I could confidently identify as the reason was this stupid glimmer of hope that if I saw the dozens of photos he'd posted before falling asleep, I might dream of him. Dreams were the safest place where he and I could be together. Dreams were the only place where it would ever happen. And I wasn't asking for much; I just wanted to sit on the grass with him, lean my back against his, let our heads touch, and tell him it feels exactly as I always dreamed it would.

Before I left his page, I opened our chat. It was a sad affair. We'd sent each other texts on birthdays and holidays and in between quick confirmations of time and place whenever I was supposed to join him and Elle for a night out. In the entire history of our texts, there wasn't a single sentence that would connect us. There had never even been a hint, yet I couldn't put him out of my mind.

Me: Thanks for helping me. It's a good book.

I sent the text, locked my phone, crossed my arms, and closed my eyes. The images I'd just looked at floated in front of my eyes. The latest one was from seven weeks ago because Gabriel's social media profiles were a ghost-town. And that one was with Elle in a cafe at the beach. The most exciting part of that photo was the fact that Gabriel was shirtless in it. But the photo was cropped just below his shoulders, so I needed to use my imagination to fill out the rest. My imagination was going wild.

When my phone buzzed, I scrambled to pick it up. And sure enough, it was from Gabriel.

Gabriel: You're welcome. I'm glad you like it. I've got tons more.

Me: Awesome. I was gonna ask you for recs.

Gabriel: Elle told me. We can work something out.

Me: Told you what?

Gabriel: The tutoring. I'm looking forward to it.

I frowned and read that message three times without understanding it. Then, I phoned Elle. She picked up after the first ring. "Little bro," she said in a way of greeting.

"Two minutes, Elle. Two minutes between us." I swallowed a grunt.

"Still makes me older," she said with the sort of pride that would make you think it was all her effort and achievement. "You're too young to understand." She gave a hearty laugh that infected me and I joined it. "What's up?" she asked after a moment.

"Did you, perhaps, in your infinite wisdom, arrange some sort of tutoring for me?" I asked. My throat threatened to close and turn my voice embarrassingly high-pitched. The mere thought of spending more time with Gabriel than was necessary made the hairs on my arms rise.

"I might have," she said quizzically.

"That's not an answer," I pointed out. "Did you?"

He sighed. "Gabriel is smart. He's reliable. He can help you pass that crap with flying colors."

I swallowed the knot in my throat. "I don't need flying colors and I can pass on my own, thank you very much."

"Swallow your pride, little bro. You need help and I have the perfect solution." Her voice grew commanding by the end of that.

"Thanks, but no thanks. I can manage on my own," I said. Putting me in the same room as Gabriel, making me sit next to him, confining us together so that he would look at me and explain things to me and move his pretty lips around while doing the said explaining, was akin to medieval torture.

"If you can pass it on your own, then why are you retaking it?" she asked.

"Touché." I bit my lip hard in thought. "You could have asked me first."

"You'll understand when you're my age, youngling," she said whimsically and laughed. "But seriously, if I asked, would you have agreed?"

"No," I admitted.

"And there you go. You're growing up as we speak." She followed that with another bubble of laughter, then sighed. "He's a smart guy, London. Give him a chance."

My soul was hollow. Yeah, Gabriel was a smart guy. *I'll gladly give him all the chances he wants, but that's like stabbing you in the back and twisting the dagger slowly.* "Will do," I said instead.

"Good boy," she said and hung up.

I opened the messages with Gabriel after leaving him hanging and found a new one from him. My heart beat faster when I read it.

Gabriel: Is tomorrow around three okay?

I checked the time. That was in fifteen hours. In fifteen hours, I would be all alone with the guy I was trying to dream about. And I would need to pretend everything was fine.

Fuck. My. Life.

This wasn't going to be easy, but I couldn't stifle the excitement of being around him. I couldn't stop thinking about staying alone with him. Underneath the fear, I was thrilled. In just fifteen hours, his deep green-brown eyes wouldn't be just in my memory, but present and gazing at me as I struggled to remember whatever formula he wanted to teach me.

Me: Perfect. Come over here.

So long as I didn't say or do or hint at anything, we were all fine.

I swore to myself, after years of pining after him, then watching him go to Elle, that I would rather rip my heart out than speak a word of my feelings. My feelings played no part in anything. They would go away. They just had to. And for years, I succeeded in keeping my feelings quiet, so I wasn't going to start yapping about them now.

In the morning, Hudson's arrival woke me up. I'd fallen asleep with my phone still on my chest. Hudson crashed onto his bed with all his weight, then undressed half-asleep, and grumbled as he drifted away.

I decided not to disturb him. It was only seven in the morning and he had obviously not slept a wink. *You lucky devil*, I thought. Whatever he was distracting himself from, he had succeeded for another night. But maybe he wasn't distracting himself from anything; maybe I was the only one who ran around having meaningless sex just to take Gabriel off my mind.

I shrugged and got up, washed my face, brushed my teeth, and went on a hunt for breakfast. There was a great cafeteria near campus with killer waffles and even better pancakes, so I made my way there all the while my heart grew heavier.

It was a small relief that I hadn't dreamed of Gabriel last night. No matter how much I always wished for it before falling asleep, my conscience was lighter if he didn't visit me in my dreams.

I kept myself busy the entire morning. After breakfast, I jogged down to the beach, swam for a solid hour with minimal breaks, and sunbathed on the rocks until my skin, hair, and underwear were dry. Then, I made a slow climb back to campus, only to find Hudson still knocked out in his bed at two in the afternoon.

"Rise and shine, bad boy," I called.

"No," he grumbled.

"It can't have been that wild last night," I said, closing the door behind me. The room was a mess of Hudson's clothes, though he wasn't the only one to blame. A few dirty socks of mine were scattered around, too. And I didn't need Gabriel to come in and see my underwear hanging from an open drawer, either.

"It was. Now I'm letting my soul leave my body." Hudson buried his head into the pillow as I pulled the blinds up and let some sunshine into the room. "Ah! It burns!"

I laughed it off. "Seriously, man, I need you to get up."

He shot out of the bed like a bullet. "Got someone special coming? Say no more."

I snorted. "Just help me hide this mess somewhere."

He shook his head to wake himself up completely, then piled up his laundry in both hands and looked around the room as though he had no clue what to do next. "Crap," he muttered. "I'll just take this to the common room with me and sleep the rest of the day."

"Sounds like a brilliant plan. Why don't you do that right now?" I checked the time on my phone, panic creeping in.

Hudson nodded and headed for the door, then looked at me over his shoulder with a sly smile. "Lock the door when he's here. I don't need the repeat of last Christmas."

I rolled my eyes. "It's not like that. It's just Gabriel. He's coming to help me with Managerial and I don't need your stinky socks to greet him." Then, I muttered, "And you could have heard there was action here last Christmas."

Hudson laughed out loud. "Believe me, I've been careful ever since. Walking in on you like that is pretty damn dangerous." Laughing louder yet, Hudson walked out of the room. He'd made plenty of jokes like this over the last year and I couldn't blame him. I was pretty big and he couldn't believe it until he walked in on me. Something about it not matching my frame made itself very memorable in Hudson's mind.

I forgot all about him when I got a five minute warning from Gabriel. He was on his way and I paced back and forth in the room, regretting this terrible idea until he knocked.

I balled my fists and marched to the door, my entire body stiff and formal. *Show nothing*, I reminded myself. *We're just studying together. We're just studying.*

I opened the door and found myself tongue-tied. Gabriel, with his wavy, black hair and deep green-brown eyes gazed down at me. "Hey," he said.

Fuck, your voice is like a sexy purr and I want to kiss you. "Hey," I said instead. "Come in." But it took me another moment to move my feet and give him the space to walk in. *Calm down*, I hissed at myself internally.

I closed the door and paused in my footsteps, took a deep, quiet breath of air filled with Gabriel's crisp, sweet scent, swallowed a growl at my ridiculous behavior, then walked after him. He sat down on Hudson's desk chair while I sorted through my notebooks and made some space on the desks.

"Did you do anything fun last night?" I asked. The trick was to keep things casual and not personal. I neither wanted, nor needed, to know anything personal about him. As if I didn't care enough already. I would start pining after his personality traits. I was better off not knowing.

"Not really. Got back to my room after seeing Elle and played *Seeds of Soulless*," Gabriel said and laughed.

I glanced at him over one of the old notebooks I was skimming through. He was slouching, holding his hands together, rubbing his left thumb over the back of his right hand. He was all big and buff and sculpted, yet the biggest geek I knew. His high cheekbones drew my eyes and a shade of pink that touched them made my heart skip a beat. *It's just hot outside*, I told myself. *Why would he blush?* "Yeah, my sister's pretty boring. You're better off hanging out with me." I heard the words leave my lips, then quickly looked away. Giving up on finding a new notebook, I sat down at my desk and flipped to the first empty page I could find.

Gabriel shrugged. "Elle's not the boring one, believe me."

"Are you saying you are?" I teased. Teasing was my safest route. I was known for it. Nobody took me seriously. "Because I'm sure you're about to prove yourself wrong. Nothing beats lengthy conversations about advanced economical formulas."

Gabriel chuckled. "That's some exciting stuff right there." He raised a hand to scratch his arm and I couldn't help myself by looking at his biceps. Everything about this guy, from his sharp lips, to his perfectly muscled body, and down to the fact that he is as off-limits as a person could be, pushed my buttons. "And you?" he asked.

"Nothing special," I said. "Saw Josh for a bit, read that book of yours, fell asleep."

Gabriel smiled. "Then, we're perfectly matched."

Don't say stuff like that if you don't want me to tip over and crash on top of you, I thought. "Where do we start?"

Gabriel opened his backpack and pulled out four heavy books. "I stopped at the library this morning. These are sort of the starting points that talk about different mechanics of management relative to internal and external economics." He lifted one of the books and handed it to me. "This one is all about international markets and how to assess their viability before entering them. We'll get there later. I'm thinking we should just follow the curriculum. But because it's only been one week, there's not much to master, so you can gain some momentum by studying in advance." I took the book from him, frowning, but he didn't stop talking. Instead, he picked up the second one. "Now this is a really good one. It's about the internal economics of each company. It's not exactly what the course is about, but it'll give you a bunch of useful knowledge that you'll connect with everything else. All jokes aside, it's really exciting."

I laughed. "These are like six million pages each," I pointed out.

Gabriel frowned like he didn't understand my meaning, then lit up. It clicked, apparently. He pushed his hands into his backpack and produced four dog-eared notebooks with a massively proud grin on his face. And frankly, even if the weight of the books he'd brought over to me was excruciating, seeing that goofy smile made my whole day. Hell, it made my week. "I've got you covered," he said.

I'd uncover myself for you right this instant, you grinning genius. "What's that?" I asked instead.

Even more proudly, Gabriel set the notebooks on my desk and opened the first one. Inside, the pages were filled with definitions, formulas, graphs, and charts. But it wasn't the main pages that blew me away. It was the margins. Every few lines, there was a note on the margins, marking the shorthand title of the book he drew from as well as the page. In some cases, he even marked paragraphs. "This way, you can see what I found was the most important. You can learn all this and get a solid grade. *But*, you can also check for more information in each book, if you want flying colors."

I stared at the pot of gold. "Holy crap, I could kiss you now."

Gabriel jerked his hands back and made a strangled sound.

I laughed out loud to cover my embarrassment. Of all the great things I could have said, this one was low on the list. "I'm not gonna," I said, then added, "But I could. Big difference."

Gabriel laughed, but it was forced. I'd embarrassed him, too. "Let's just read this, huh?"

"Good thinking," I said. "Kissing's overrated." *Why can't I fucking shut up?*

And just like that, my glance met his gaze, and time stopped. I could see myself leaning in and letting my lips brush lightly against his. I could see myself breaking all our hearts just to feel the warmth of his face near mine. I could see myself never recovering from this. Destroying my family and hurting my sister, destroying her relationship, and making Gabriel hate me. And the fool that I was, I couldn't categorically say it wouldn't be worth it.

Gabriel licked his red lips and pulled back, slouching once again.

This disaster was averted, but my heart pumped blood into my body at an alarming rate. We were merely ten minutes into our first session and I was already close to wrecking all the lives that mattered to me.

"You said we should follow the curriculum," I pointed out, barely louder than a whisper. I was desperate for a change of topic.

"Yes, but if you start early, then you'll..."

I cut in. "No, I mean... You want to tutor me the entire semester?"

Gabriel frowned. "Uh, sure. That's the idea."

My throat was seizing and I worked like hell to bring my pulse down.

"It's really not an easy subject, London. You know that by now. Tons of people flunked." He was careful with his words. He was reserved.

"Why would you spend your free time helping me? It's not like you need money. Am I even paying you?"

He chuckled, but it was as forced as a person could make it. "You're right. I don't. And you're not. I...uh...want to help you."

My eyes narrowed. "But why?"

Gabriel gave a jerky shake of his head. "It's not pity. Don't worry. I just... I have known you since I was a kid. You're Elle's brother. Who else should I help?"

"But you could be with her. Instead, you're spending your Saturday helping me. We've never really been friends despite knowing each other." *Why exactly was I sabotaging this?* Anger at myself began to lurk in the depths of my soul.

"We could be," he said softly. "It's not too late."

"What? Friends? We could be friends without you doing me a massive favor," I said.

Gabriel backed even further away from me. His shiny green-brown eyes shone a little less. "Do you want me to help you or not?" he asked bluntly.

"I do. I really do. But I thought it was just once or twice and didn't feel that bad. But I can't ask you

to sacrifice all your free time to help a lost cause."
I shrugged. This was as honest as I dared be.

Gabriel used his toes to drag the desk chair on
its wheels closer to me. "You're not a lost cause,
London."

"You know what I mean," I said.

He shook his head. "I don't mind spending my
free time with you. Besides, Elle and I see each
other plenty and it was her idea. She won't miss
me."

"And you won't miss her," I said. It was supposed
to be a joke, but it didn't come out quite right.

Gabriel gave a slow, sad shrug. "Plenty of time,"
he said.

"I just don't want you to be forced to do any
favors," I said. "It's not fair."

He gave me a long look that I could not decipher
if my life depended on it. "I want to do this."

I rubbed my hands as silence lingered between
us a few moments longer. "Let's do it, then."

It seemed to be that easy to make Gabriel light
up again. He lost himself in the notes he'd written
two years earlier within a couple of heartbeats.
For two hours, he spoke of the basic principles
of economics, even answering stupid questions
such as, "When will I ever need to know this?" or
statements like, "I'm so lost right now." Patiently,
he spoke on and on and on, somehow referencing
The Lord of the Rings three solid times throughout
the lessons.

He was such an adorable nerd — and hot as fuck,
for the love of God — that I had to force myself to
listen carefully, or else I would lose myself in the
dreamland where nothing aside from his pretty

lips existed. Every time he bobbed his head in thought after I'd asked a question, I watched the beating pulse in his neck and wondered what his skin tasted like.

For two hours, I suffered the sweetest, cruelest pain. On one hand, he was a guy I'd been crushing on since I was a kid. On the other hand, here was my sister's boyfriend of two years.

And if that math hadn't broken my heart time and time again, nothing ever had. Because I'd had a crush on him *first*.

CHAPTER THREE

Cucumber

FOR AN ENTIRE WEEK, I successfully forgot all about London. Not only that, but I had seen Elle the night before the next tutoring session, kissed her, and it had all gone smoothly. I'd kissed her without a panic attack.

The only time when I thought of London this past week had been when I made a mind-map of the basic constructs of Managerial Economics that I thought would help him understand the connections better. By the time I'd finished the maps, I had forgotten all about London, and was writing down formula breakdowns for the fun of it.

Now, I checked the time, saved my progress on *Seeds of Soulless*, and stuffed the folder with maps and formulas inside my backpack. London was on my mind again and it was strangely comforting as much as it was wildly unsettling.

I couldn't wash away the taste of my panic attack. And, as I walked across the lawn between our dormitories, the taste only intensified.

Last Saturday had been hard enough, sitting next to him and pretending I hadn't thought of kissing him while holding Elle in my arms. My brain had gone into a minor meltdown by the time the session was over. The only thing that had kept me sane — ridiculous as it might sound — was the math I was explaining to him.

I got to London's room and knocked on the door. The sound of running water was muffled by two doors, and so was the voice. "Come in," he called faintly.

I walked into the room all the while my nerves were glowing like embers. My brows were already sweaty from the heat outside, but it only got worse. The room was empty. London was in the bathroom.

"I'll just be a minute," he said from the shower.

My heart tripped and I sat down. The office chair spun and I closed my eyes. Images of London showering six feet away from me were not welcome and did not reach my brain. Not the conscious part of it, at least. I had no business thinking about that. And even if I were to imagine these things, they were merely a product of my curiosity. Nothing more.

London turned the water off and I heard him humming. Moments passed; I wiped my palms against my knee-length shorts, and stilled my heart the best I could. It wouldn't rest; it just wouldn't.

And I didn't know why.

But it nearly jumped out of my chest when the bathroom door creaked open and London, water dripping from his hair, tip-toed out in nothing but a big bath towel tied around his waist.

"He-he, I've seen a certain movie starting this way," he said.

I swallowed the knot in my pulsing throat. "What movie?" I asked absentmindedly.

London waved his hand in dismissal. "You wouldn't know it." He found it funny, but all I was aware of was the broadness of his shoulders as he turned away from me. A drop of water slid down between his shoulder blades and my mouth went dry.

I held my breath as the room spun around my mind.

London picked up a pair of black boxer-briefs with small pineapples dotted all over it, stepped inside of them, and dragged them up his legs and under the towel. They went out of my sight, but I could picture every inch of his legs as he slid the underwear up.

Swiftly, he untied the towel and pulled it away like a magician who was about to stun the audience with his apprentice's impossible disappearance. His muscles twisted as he turned halfway around.

I held my breath still as I stared at his full-body profile. I'd seen him shirtless countless times in the past. I've seen him in his underwear now and then, too. Yet it had never done this to me before. It had never made my body rock inside and out.

Nobody had ever done *this* to me.

His butt — *stop looking at his butt!* — was firm, somehow tight, in those boxer-briefs, and his...ah, front was...*something*. I tore my gaze off his lower half only to find his firm abs, smooth, creamy skin with a natural summer tan, and beads of water still sprinkled on him.

He twisted his torso again, flexing the muscles of his back, as he searched for a pair of shorts and a T-shirt to throw on.

And when he bent over to put the shorts on, my heart wanted to explode. His butt looked a little bigger now, but just as firm. The curve was almost too much to look at.

Lightheaded, I grabbed the edge of the desk to keep myself still. "Crap, I... I forgot I have a... Thing." I shot to my feet and found the discomforting ache in my pants. The pressure was immense as my cock grew harder, and it grew quickly. "Promised Andy and forgot. I'll uh... I'll make it up to you. Text me when you're free." I blurted all the words at once as I passed by him and headed for the door.

"Gabriel, your backpack," London said.

I spun around, grabbed the backpack from the chair, and headed out.

I stormed across the lawn that separated our dormitories. It was a wonder I managed to walk up the stairs with my jelly legs and shaking knees. I burst into my room, shut the door, turned the key, and crashed onto my bed, still shaking.

I just got hard for London. London, a guy, not a location, though that would be equally weird. London, my girlfriend's brother. London...

My cock throbbed as I fought tooth and nail to purge the memory of his ass out of my head.

I'd gone without sex for too long I was starting to see London as Elle. That had to be it.

It had to.

Otherwise...

Nope. I am not going there. I turned on my bed and found the joystick I'd thrown there on my way out. As quickly and nimbly as if I were fighting a soulless, I entered my game and lost myself in the epic music and first-class rendering of the open fantasy world. It was my sanctuary. Or it seemed so, because London found a way to creep in there, too.

My heart pounded as I ran through the devastated wilderness of the game world, but it also pounded because of London.

I paused the game, unable to distract myself with it. Instead, I undressed messily and walked into the bathroom Andy and I shared, let the water run, and stepped under. It was cold, just the way I needed it. It chilled me to my bones, the contrast between my heated body and the freezing cold water sharpening my senses for a few steady moments.

I closed my eyes and pressed the tip of my head against the tiled wall, then took slow, deep breaths of air to bring my pulse down.

Minutes passed and I shivered, but not because of the cold. Not entirely, at least.

I poured a bunch of body wash on my open palm and started to rub it over my body. I kept my eyes closed as I did this, wincing at the occasional sprinkle of cold water that reached me.

Every muscle in my body was tense. Every cell was confused. Every nerve ending was aflame.

I rubbed my chest and arms and armpits, my back, my abs. Then, I reached for my cock, and holy fuck, it got hard again. Nothing I did seemed to do the trick and I'd be damned if I gave in and rubbed it out.

My hands abandoned my half-upright cock before I did something else with the thoughts of the inexplicable and moved to my ass. I rubbed the body wash over my cheeks and, as my fingers reached between, I held my breath.

Don't do it.

Don't you fucking do it.

Don't!

My index finger circled my hole and curiosity, no matter how life-wrecking, overpowered me. The tip of my finger pressed my hole and I clenched, but in an instant, I relaxed my hole, and my finger entered me.

The burning cold sensation I attributed to the body wash on my finger was negligible compared to the inflation of my chest and the instant, rapid rise of my cock.

I jerked my hand away and slammed an open palm against the tiled wall. "Ah, fuck," I moaned as my hole quickly clenched and relaxed, again and again. My cock throbbed harder and I shifted and stood under the showerhead. The water washed the soap off my body and I absently rubbed my legs clean, too, but my mind was spinning. My soul was leaving my body and traversing the great expanse beyond the observable universe.

"Fuck," I whispered, far less ecstatically than be-fore, and with a lot more disappointment.

My racing heart couldn't speed up anymore.

Though I was more mature than any of my friends, at the age of twenty-two, I never consid-ered myself too old for anything. But this, man... This... I was too fucking old to discover *this*.

It's no big deal, I told myself as I stepped out of the shower and dried myself numbly. I stared at the mirror, but I was looking through it. *Men have prostates and this can happen. It means nothing. Nothing. It's just a kink of anatomy.*

Except, if my memory served me well — which it definitely fucking did — then I knew there was no way I'd even gotten close to that spot.

Don't think about it, Gabriel.

My chest heaved as I dressed in panic and stormed out of the bathroom. I paced the room wearing nothing but a pair of shorts, sweat break-ing out all over my torso.

As if questioning everything I thought I'd known about myself wasn't enough, this just had to be triggered by the single, worst possible person in the world. Of all the people, it just had to be Lon-don.

I closed my eyes and leaned against the desk under the window. London... He wasn't the worst at anything. He was a really sweet guy, but I did not need him in my thoughts like this. He was the very last guy I needed, were I to need *any* guy.

So why was I sad?

Why the fuck did the idea of pushing all of this down and erasing it from my memory make me this fucking inconsolable?

Letting go of the thoughts that had sent me running away from London was like severing a limb for no reason. It was like giving up something important, but without a reward.

I didn't want to let go of this fantasy. But I had to.

And when my stomach growled to warn me I needed to eat, my absurd dilemma only worsened. I walked out of the room and into our small, shared kitchen, opened the fridge, and lost the last breath of air from my lungs. This one item in the fridge left me suffocating, fighting for air while I had to fight the creeping thoughts.

A cucumber.

A long, slender cucumber.

A phallic cucumber.

"No," I muttered. "Shut up. Just, shut up." I grabbed a tomato, a bit of lettuce, humus, sun-dried tomatoes in olive oil, and a pepper. I sliced it all on the cutting board, spread the humus on a slice of bread, and put together a decent sandwich. Then, I stormed back to my room with the determination of Sisyphus to forget all about the cucumber and just eat my sandwich in silence. I might play my game and put London out of my mind, too. I should. Until today, it had never failed to immerse me fully.

But as soon as I ate my sandwich, my insides twisted and longing filled my heart. There was a part of me that was burning with curiosity and I knew — I fucking knew — that saying it was just my scientific brain being curious was a lie, but I still stood up and walked back to the fridge.

With a shaking hand and a dry mouth, I picked up the cucumber and glanced around to make sure nobody was looking. It was smooth and damn cold, but even thinking about holding it turned my heart into a fluttering mess.

I rushed back into my room, locked the door, threw the cucumber on my bed and spun away from it. *I am not seriously going to do this, am I?* But I needed to know. The want for knowledge was burning in me with the brightness of a blacksmith's forge. And I wasn't fooling myself, either. It was not only the pure, detached scientific need for information.

It went far deeper than that.

And nobody needed to know.

Only I needed to know.

I sat down at the edge of my bed, rested my hands in my lap, and breathed steadily as the cucumber lay idly, uselessly three feet away from me. My hands shook nervously, but it wasn't from fear. I was cool enough by now to know the shaking for what it was. It was pure thrill too.

I didn't want to like this, but I also did.

Biting my lip, I pushed myself up, crossed the room to the wardrobe, and dug around for my supplies. An old pack of condoms, barely opened, was there. Lube, used a lot more often, was also there. All I needed now was courage. But my aching erection hinted that I wasn't too far away from the final decision.

No matter how much I wanted to forget all about this, I couldn't. I'd already discovered something that had never crossed my mind and I was set on my course.

I dragged my shorts and underwear down my legs, lay on my back, and closed my eyes. Unsurprisingly, it was the image of London that floated in front of my eyes and sent all my blood down to my cock.

I was rock hard when I wrapped my fingers around the shaft and gave a slow, gentle stroke along the length. Even thinking of doing this sent a wave of shivers down my spine and filled my chest with fearful excitement.

I tightened my grip around my cock and stopped moving my hand along the length. Instead, I held it, feeling pulse after excited pulse as my other hand sought the mistake I was about to make. *It is a mistake, but it's such a thrilling mistake that I cannot go back. I cannot just pretend this never happened. I cannot just decide to stop and never wonder what it would be like.*

This would be my little secret. I would take it to my grave if I had to, but it needed to happen.

I abruptly let go of my cock. It slapped against my lower abdomen as I unwrapped a condom and slipped it down the length of the cucumber. My heart skip-skip-skipped every other or third beat.

I put a few drops of lube on top and realized my mouth was watering. Fear gave way to excitement the more I slicked my improvised dildo and I nearly forgot about everything else. The thrill of doing something so secret and so wildly different coursed through my veins as I bent my legs, pushed my feet into the mattress, and aimed the cucumber where I shouldn't — but desperately wanted to.

When the sheathed tip of it touched my crack, I shivered and almost changed my mind. *Almost*. I took a deep breath of air and held it, biting the inside of my lower lip and closing my eyes. My biceps tensed; my abs flexed. I pushed the thing in ruthlessly and carelessly, thinking it was better to just be done with it. My cock throbbed and straightened, but pain whitened my mind and I cried out. I hadn't even gotten it in and it was already too much.

I dropped the cucumber right away and opened my eyes to stare at the blank ceiling. The pain faded away from my pulsing hole, leaving only an oddly warm tingling sensation. But that was the least of what I felt. The other thing was bitter disappointment.

By right, I shouldn't have been disappointed. I should have gotten up and celebrated that it had all just been a lapse of my mind. Some odd curiosity that wouldn't leave me alone had gotten me here, and now, I was free of it. I knew it for a fact. I did not like this.

I heaved breath after breath as sweat slicked my bare torso. My cock was still hard and I was still horny as fuck, but I wasn't sure if I wanted to do anything else.

As my breathing returned to normal, my disappointment only grew. As silly as it might have been, I nurtured a sliver of hope. Even if it was only inside my head, I still felt that glimmer of hope that there might be more to life and love and lust than what I had.

As inevitable as tax collection, London's face emerged from the mist of my mind. His cheek-

bones and his shoulders with drops of water after a shower, his defined chest and abs, his firm
butt packed so tightly in the boxer-briefs. All these
fragments of him floated through my mind and
made themselves as clear as if he was standing in
front of me. As if he was lying on top of me.

My chest squeezed hard and I reached down
with my left hand, still slick with lube. I touched
my taint and felt the rush of excitement rise to my
chest. My index finger traced my taint indepen-
dently of my mind. It followed my desire, but not
my logic or my rational wishes. Perhaps I should
have been satisfied with failing to toy with the
cucumber, but I wasn't. I still knew, deep down,
there was something I wanted here.

My finger circled my rim, soothed the ache that
was, by now, purely imaginary. The warm and
stinging sensation was subtle as I tuned my mind
and my feelings. I realized, after a few seconds of
massaging myself, that my hole was pulsing just
as much as my dick. Waiting for a moment of
relaxation, I rubbed and increased pressure. And
when it came, it all happened instantly.

My finger slipped inside painlessly, well lubed
and rather thinner than a cucumber, which was
thinner still than my dick. But the moment my
finger entered me, my dick loved it. It shot upright
and stayed like that, my hole tightening around
my knuckle. A moan of surprise dragged out of my
parted lips and my eyes rolled back in my skull.
I pushed my head deeper into the pillow, needy
for something or someone to hold me like this. I
wished for a nicely sculpted body to lay on top of
me this very instant, to press down on me, to reach

for my hand and help me finger myself. I wished for it so much that I could taste the strawberry which I imagined London's lips tasted like.

A shivering breath of air entered my lungs as I pulled my finger out, then pushed it back in. Each fraction of movement made my cock jerk and I wrapped my right hand around it to hold it still. Each move my finger made was easier. They were so easy, in fact, that after a few long, careful minutes of playing around, I was sliding it in and out the same way I was sliding my right hand along the length of my dick.

The tip of my cock was slick with precum, dripping and more plentiful than I'd ever seen it. Somewhere in the back of my mind, I wondered if it was solely because of what I was doing with my finger.

As I sped up, I grew lustier and braver. I slowed down almost to a stop and carefully pressed my middle finger at my entrance, then pushed. Two fingers were harder to take, but I would be damned if I quit now. They stretched me slowly and just like before, it became easier after a few minutes. At times, I held my breath and bit my tongue to hold back the moans. Someone passing down the hallway and overhearing me wouldn't be the most ideal situation to be in.

But I fucking loved it. I loved every searing moment of it.

Abruptly, I pulled my fingers out and poured lube over my open palm, snatched the cucumber, and made sure the upper third of it was well covered. That had to do the trick.

Holding it with both hands, the long and slender thing that it was, I pressed it hard against my hole and waited. Seconds ticked away but I couldn't make my body relax. Not quite so quickly. Instead, I waited for the tension to pass. First, my abs relaxed a little. Then, the muscles in my legs and arms loosened. And finally, my cock rested on my abdomen and my hole relaxed.

Gently, now, I applied pressure to the covered cucumber and felt its first fraction of an inch enter me. It was bigger and thicker than my two fingers, but not by much. Still, it felt totally different. My hole accepted it, got used to it, and I pushed a little harder. But only a little; not at all as manically as I had originally.

The moment in which the tip of the cucumber pushed through the tight entrance, stars spilled in front of my closed eyes. These were definitely the good kind because my cock stiffened and my hole tightened, but I could still push deeper in. Painless as it was, the sensation was unlike anything I'd ever imagined. It was unique to this act alone.

But even then, I hadn't been able to ever imagine the feeling of what came next. Because now, as I pushed and pulled and quickened the pace and explored myself freely and deeper, the cucumber reached in and pressed against the spot that made me whimper with excruciating pleasure. The itch that emerged was somewhere deep inside of me, but I knew, by instinct, that gripping my cock would help it. With my right hand, I stroked myself mercilessly. With my left, I gripped the cucumber and rammed it into myself, hoping to push that button again.

Whether it was the moment when I thrust my hips up, then dragged them down or the moment when I tilted the cucumber so that the other end of it was pressed against the mattress, I didn't know. It didn't matter. What mattered was that my mind spun and the cucumber was repeatedly pushing against my prostate, sending wave after burning wave of stinging tingles through my entire body.

My right hand quickened and my cock throbbed harder than ever. Cum shot out in fucking buckets as an orgasm thundered through me. I shook and shivered and persisted, pressing my prostate only to make my cock twitch harder. Drops of cum fell onto my chest and my sweat-covered abs as I opened my mouth wide and let the air flow in and out of me.

"What the fuck was that?" I whispered to myself, eyes still closed, mouth hanging open. I winced as I pulled the cucumber out, my hole sore and throbbing. Warmth spilled through my insides once the cucumber was out and I stayed in the bed for a long while, savoring the sensation.

Though I thought, briefly, how I'd now done it and never had to do it again, I knew that those were lies. This feeling... It was addictive. Even thinking about never trying this again — even on my own, without ever telling a soul — saddened me. I knew I couldn't give it up.

But I had some thinking to do. For fuck's sake, I had some serious thinking to do. Would this affect my life? Would I let it? Could I keep it down?

The worst of it all, I had an urge to find someone and tell them. I wanted to tell London most of all. If anyone would understand, he would. He wouldn't tell on me, either. He wouldn't out me to my dad. His words wouldn't disinherit me.

But I didn't dare tell him. He would hate my guts for stabbing Elle in the back. And Elle... I couldn't... *I can't...but I have to tell her.*

Yet, as I rested and regained my breath, it was London who I wanted to have here. It was London who I wanted to wrap my arms around and hold in silence. It was London who I wanted to share this feeling with.

CHAPTER FOUR

Ripped Apart

_____ele_____

"YEAH?" I GOT OUT of the bed, leaving Gabriel's notebook open, and headed for the door. "Hudson, if you forgot the key again…" I turned the knob and forgot the rest of what I was about to say.

It wasn't Hudson. It was Gabriel. He had his hands behind his back and an apologetic smile on his handsome face.

"Oh," I heard myself saying. "What's up?"

"I'm sorry I bailed on you today," he said. "Here." He moved his left arm from behind his back and revealed a book-shaped package wrapped in gift paper topped with a little bow.

I took the package in my hand and turned it around. "Um…you didn't have to get me anything."

Gabriel shrugged. "I felt bad."

"Dude, you had other plans. We're cool."

He shrugged once again.

In silence, I tore the gift paper off and pulled out a thick paperback book. *Micro to Macro: Economics Explained*, said the title. "Wow," I said. "How did you know?" My sarcasm often went far enough that it could be mistaken for truth.

But Gabriel laughed so hard that his shoulders shook. "See? I listen."

An alternative universe, in which a life I'd never lived, flashed in front of my eyes. In that universe, Elle had never liked Gabriel. In that universe, Gabriel was into guys and he wasn't ashamed of it. He'd made it clear to everyone and he only had eyes for me. In that universe, Gabriel listened to my wishes.

Why do you have to say things like this? I didn't ask. "Lucky Elle," I whispered and flipped through the book, then cleared my throat. "Wanna come in?"

"Door frame's totally fine," Gabriel said.

I snorted. "Come on." I moved to the side and let him through. "But don't get any ideas..."

He spun his head so quickly that I stopped mid-sentence. Whatever I'd said scared the crap out of him. "What?"

I made a brief pause, then finished my sentence. "...we're not studying tonight."

The fright in his eyes went away as quickly as it had come. "Oh. Oh, right. Totally. Sure. No studying."

I squinted. "Are you alright?"

"Why?" he asked and sat at the very edge of Hudson's chair, hands on his knees. There was tension in his broad shoulders and pinkness in his cheeks. His dark hair was short and wavy and his cheeks were lightly covered with a five o'clock shade. Glancing at it was enough to make me wonder what it would feel like to kiss him. Would my skin burn from his short beard? Where else would that sensation rock my world? *Stop it*, I told myself and pushed the image of Gabriel doing some unspeakable things to me, his beard searing the smooth and soft parts of my skin that rarely saw the sun.

I shuddered, but forced myself to calm down. *I need a distraction*. "How about we grab drinks instead?" I scratched the back of my head and found Gabriel's eyes leaving my gaze and locking onto my arm. I felt exposed, for a moment. But he quickly looked at me and I missed the feeling that he might — just might — be looking at me. "I'll go crazy, holed up in here."

"Drinks sounds great," he said and licked his lips.

"Lemme change real quick," I said and dropped the book onto my bed, then opened my wardrobe. Gabriel spun in the chair and gazed outside as I shed my clothes off and put on something nicer. Not once did he seem to even notice my movements. It was completely unlike what had happened today; and that one stuck with me, though I couldn't quite put my finger on why.

Once done, I cleared my throat, and Gabriel spun back in the chair with an innocent expression on his face. "Any destination in mind?" he asked.

"Whichever serves beer," I said. The day had been hot and my thirst had only grown. It grew even more so since Gabriel's unexpected arrival, but that sort of thirst could not be quenched by beer.

For weeks, I'd lost all interest in my regular anonymous hookups. For weeks, I couldn't put him out of my mind. Whatever the reason, he was present in my thoughts more than ever before. It was the opposite of what I'd hoped would happen. I'd hoped, for ages now, that it would just go away.

If only I could erase him from my mind, I could finally live. Not a moment before.

Gabriel got up and we headed outside. The heat of the evening caught me by surprise, after spending most of the day in an air-conditioned room.

My hand slipped gently under my loose and billowy T-shirt and felt my abs. It was a habit I rarely thought of. Some guys adjusted their dicks all the time, never seeming to notice it. Me? I felt my abs. I felt them good. But on this particular occasion, Gabriel's gaze dropped to where I was partially lifting my T-shirt, and he swallowed hard, then looked away with force.

We walked across campus and he seemed to be trying to say something, but his voice was strangled and he only produced a couple of murmurs.

"Huh?" I glanced at him casually. Playing cool and stupid was my ultimate talent.

He cleared his throat. "Can I ask you something?"

"I need to think on it," I said.

He snorted. "We used to be close," he said. "As kids. We used to play together all the time."

"Uh-huh." I didn't like where this line of thinking was going and I prepared the mental bricks and mortar to put up the wall in case he came too close.

"What happened?" He shook his head as if he couldn't believe that, in the last ten or so years, we never became friends.

I fell in love with you. He'd been climbing a tree that summer. He'd been wearing blue shorts and nothing else. It had been innocent enough; I'd been eleven, Gabriel thirteen. He'd reached with his left foot for a higher branch and his shorts dragged a little higher up. In an instant, he looked down from the tree and grinned mischievously at me, a naughty spark twinkling in his eyes. And that had done it for me. I stood there, mouth hanging open, as a million little needles pricked my skin and realization seeped through. I had realized *everything*; about myself, about Gabriel, about the world. It had been the moment I left my childhood behind and understood it all.

Years had gone on and I had coped with it on my own. Quickly, I had learned that being around Gabriel always made me sad. For the first time ever, I'd looked in the mirror for a long while, and muttered the words 'I'm gay.' Then, I realized there was a conversation I needed to have with my parents.

"London?" Gabriel's husky voice pulled me from my memories.

I shrugged. "People drift apart, man."

Every sleepover had been a hell. Every group vacation had hurt. I'd been in love with Gabriel since that day and it had never gone away. The flame had only grown. The older we got, the more attracted to him I had become. And then, as the world started thinking of us as all grown up, ready to face the world, the flame was so bright and hot that it turned stone to lava.

It was supposed to go away, right? People should be able to get over someone, correct?

And you just had to be straight. You just had to go a step further and date my sister too.

We turned left and climbed down the hill from Highgate to the strip. To my left was an endless row of bars and restaurants of all shapes, sizes, types, and qualities. Since I had no preference whatsoever, I gestured towards the first one that had some empty tables by the protective railing. They all had an ocean view and most of them were hanging over the water, too.

Gabriel followed. "Why did we drift, though?" he asked. It didn't sound like he directed the question at me at all. But the question was hanging between us and one had to bite the bait.

I sighed. "I dunno, man. We both made other friends along the way." I snorted softly. "It's not like we're out of time." *But I can't be friends with you. Not ever.* Having a round of drinks was one thing, but telling him my thoughts and feelings, texting him beyond birthday wishes, or going to him with all my highs and lows was not an option.

The further away from Gabriel I was, the safer. So long as I felt this unbearable pull toward him, I would never break free. Even the lessons, even seeing him with Elle, even this round of drinks was just another little stab at my bruised and beaten heart.

I knew I had to stop seeing him altogether to finally free myself of loving him. Yet I couldn't resist picking at the stitches that barely kept my heart whole.

We lounged in the corner closest to the ocean and I lost myself in my thoughts, my gaze somewhere distant, watching the endless shifting of the water and the steady, unstoppable rolling of the waves. There was only space for two chairs, so we sat at a ninety-degree angle from one another. One wrong move of my arm would allow me to feel his skin on mine. One long sigh would send my breath into his lungs. One clumsy bump would ruin our lives.

"Can I ask you something else?" Gabriel said, voice falling low. "It's, uh, personal."

I bit my lip to suppress a sneaky smile. "Full of questions, are we?" He chuckled at that. "Eh, I guess. So long as you're not quizzing me on Managerial."

His smile carried warmth that matched his big, green-brown eyes. "What was it like? I mean, when you realized you were gay."

I blew out a long breath of air. He might as well have asked me to catch up on the last ten years in a few short sentences. And where would I even begin? What would I say and what would I leave out? One wrong, miscalculated thought could out my feelings in a heartbeat.

I could see Elle's heart shattering. I could see Gabriel feeling sick. I could see myself walking away never to return. Somewhere cold and grim and lonely.

"My parents are cool," I said. "Coming out isn't easy, but I know I had it easier than most folks. Even if I was afraid of telling them, they had this whole 'unconditional love' thing going on since we were kids." I shrugged. "I think Elle knew before I said anything."

Gabriel's eyebrows danced.

"We can't read each other's minds," I said with a laugh.

"But you can feel it," he said. It was almost a question, but not quite.

It was also an excuse for me to talk about something else. "It's not even a clear feeling. Okay, so imagine someone kicking a puppy..."

"Jesus, London," Gabriel said with a disgusted frown and a cringe expression.

"Exactly. It's like what you just felt. You don't actually feel the kick but it's like your empathy is heightened. So, let's say you and Elle are both sad. I can feel for you both the way one human feels for another. But I'm definitely gonna feel for her more. If she's hurt, empathy will rip my chest open even if I don't exactly feel the literal, physical sensation. It's just the way it's always been. Also, the puppy's totally fine. A happy family adopted the puppy and it's unharmed and totally imaginary." I laughed with Gabriel.

Just in time, our drinks arrived. I was fearing he was loading a new question, one that would strike even closer to my heart.

We lifted our glasses simultaneously and both took a long sip. When Gabriel put his beer down, his upper lip was white with foam and I choked. His tongue slipped briefly and cleaned the foam, as well as it took my breath away.

"Did you always know, though?" he asked abruptly.

"About the puppy being imaginary? Sure. I made it up." I played a fool and he saw through it. His gaze lingered on me. "I dunno, man. When I was really young, like six or seven, I kinda had this weird feeling in my chest whenever I saw hand-some guys. I used to think I was intimidated by them until later, when I figured there was more to it."

"So there was, like, an *aha* moment," Gabriel said with a nod.

"Are you doing research or questioning your-self?" I teased.

His eyes widened and he licked his lips quickly, then looked away. "Just curious. We never talked about it."

My frown came and went before he noticed. "It was never a big deal for me. Not like for guys who aren't sure if they'll get beaten and thrown out of their homes."

Gabriel avoided my eyes and he closed his hand around the glass of beer, then gulped down a cou-ple of mouthfuls.

My chest tittered and a drop of sweat tickled me as it dragged between my shoulder-blades, right down my spine.

I leaned back and gazed out, sipping my beer slowly. Gabriel was quiet for a long while, which I didn't mind. It was better than walking on eggshells that were my answers to his questions.

"If I were questioning myself, you'd be the one to ask," he said and chuckled, though I couldn't quite believe it was a genuine laugh. Something about it was forced.

Then, he looked into my eyes and I all but lost it. His pupils dilated and his cheeks were red and he was exactly as he had always been in my dreams. Even the beating of his heart was visible in his long neck.

I forced a laugh even more fake than his own. "Right. Maybe after you and Elle tie the knot."

He laughed at that. "Right." His entire body shrunk. He fell in on himself. Slouching and looking down, he was infinitely smaller than the sculpted boulder he usually was. "You two are so alike," he murmured.

I snorted.

"Sorry. I know, I know, you don't want to hear it, but..." He shrugged. "It's just the way it is." He fell quiet and I listened to my own heartbeat. The silence lingered forever and it hung heavy. Something had to happen. The longer we were quiet, the grander the release needed to be. And just then, Gabriel looked up, chest inflating as he took a deep breath, fear crawling into his eyes. His arm brushed against mine and sent icicles into my heart. "London, I..." His lips parted and he stared at me like I was a ghost.

But I stared back at him just the same. "Don't say anything," I whispered, fear shooting through my chest and making my head spin.

The desperation on his face was telling enough.

"Whatever it is, don't tell me," I whispered quickly.

"Too late now," he murmured. "If I don't, I'll explode."

So, it's that. I didn't know for sure, but nothing else came to my mind. What on Earth could have made him this vulnerable and this scared? It had to be *that*.

All I ever wanted is within my reach. A clumsy bump. A sudden move.

His lip trembled, his muscles tensed. He kept his gaze on me, as if pleading for me to let him speak. And if I did? What then? Would we just elope never to be found? Would we face my sister? My family? *His dad*? "I don't need to know, Gabriel," I said, my heart's stitches tearing, ripping, snapping.

"I think you already know," he said, voice choking and trembling, but exhibiting all the bravery of a young man fighting back the tears. "I think... I'm afraid I made the wrong..."

"Choice?" I barked out a bitter laugh.

"Maybe I made a mistake," he said, voice small and frail. "What if...?"

My eyes stung, but I swore to myself I wouldn't let a tear show. "What if you got the wrong twin?" Venom laced my words. "We're not that hard to tell apart. It's subtle, but it's there. Elle's got a small birthmark under her left eye and I have a nine-inch dick."

The pinkness in Gabriel's cheeks drained until he was all deathly white. His mouth was open and his eyebrows were slowly curving into an embarrassed frown. He sucked in a breath of air, like a quiet sob, and shook his head. "London..."

"Don't," I barked and stiffened further.

"But what if I was only attracted to her because...?"

"Of me? Oh no. Don't put that on me, you lying piece of..." I couldn't make myself say it. I couldn't make myself hurt him any more than this. But I couldn't let him see my sympathy.

The wall between us rose. His openness with me ended abruptly and he straightened. His mouth closed and his eyes narrowed. He was obviously done with this shit as much as I was.

I lifted my chin in cold and ruthless defiance.

"Don't lie that it never crossed your mind," he said in his iciest voice. "You're the one who walked away from being friends. You're the one who still looks at me like a shy schoolgirl looks at boy bands. Look me in the eyes and tell me it's not what I think it is."

I shot him my coldest stare. "Whatever you think, you're wrong." My lips twitched but I forced them to calm. If only I could do the same to my shaking hands. "What is this, even? Are you coming out?" I barked the question with much more animosity than I'd wanted, but the words were already out.

"I don't know," he said in a strangled growl. "I'm fucked up and I don't know."

For the love of God, I want to help you, but I can't. "Whatever it is, it's got nothing to do with me. Got it?"

Gabriel lifted his chin high, almost like he was in front of a firing squad. He nodded.

"You should go now," I said. It took the last of my strength to say these words without showing emotions. If he only so much as stalled — let alone outright refused — I wouldn't be able to keep the act going. I would fold and crumble and slide and tell him everything. I would tell him that I'd dreamed of this moment every evening for the last ten years. I would admit that I'd hated him and Elle from afar when they first got together. I would beg him to give me a chance and tell him we could run away and leave all this mess behind.

Luckily, he jerked his chair back and stood up.

As he passed me, I croaked, "Gabriel."

He paused.

"Tell her," I said without looking back at him. "Or I'll have to." I kept my gaze safely on the horizon.

Gabriel said nothing. His silence lingered for an eternity, then his footsteps banged in my mind as he walked away.

And when I could no longer hear him, I put a hand over my mouth to stop the flood of cries and sobs from leaving me. The bubble grew infinitely in my chest and tears gathered in my eyes. The horizon blurred with the moonshine reflecting against the never-ending crashing of the waves.

I didn't breathe.

I didn't think.

I didn't move.

CHAPTER FIVE

No Looking Back

———

THE WORDS I'D SAID still rang in my ears.

What an idiot I was! To open up so carelessly and tell him the things I wasn't even sure of.

But I am *sure of one thing*, my inner voice whispered. *I'm sure I've been lying to myself.*

"Tell her," he'd said as a warning. "Or I'll have to."

I shuddered. It wasn't even the thought of London telling Elle about this that scared me. It was the way he'd said the words. It was the tired, emotionless tone that sent chills down my spine and made my eyes sting. It was the fact that I'd gotten it so wrong and thought that maybe he liked me the same way I was beginning to like him.

Because I was. When had it begun? I couldn't tell, but it was there now. It was sure as hell there and it felt familiar. It felt like I'd been carrying it with me all these years without fully knowing.

Because one look at his bare back had sent me spiraling. It had changed everything.

With a shaking hand, I pulled my phone out of my pocket. I pulled up my messages and saw that I'd texted London before the tutoring session today. His name was at the top of my list. Reading it sent a spear through my chest. If only the spear would finish me off.

I scrolled past London's text and tapped on Elle.

Me: *We need to talk. I need you. Please.*

The message went and no reply came.

If London had called her, she was probably burning all my gifts and our memories by now. I deserve no less.

I kept on walking. I walked so far out that I barely recognized the place. I'd passed the long strip and *Don Juan*, where a party was starting to rage, and climbed up the road to the plateau overlooking the cliffs and the ocean's crashing immensity. And still, I walked.

Little of my surroundings came through to my consciousness. Little did I notice.

My mind was everywhere and nowhere at the same time. Elle and London, London and Elle. And me, somewhere in between, causing it all to wreck and fall apart.

Why did he have to scratch his head that day? Why did he have to look at me so shyly? Why did he have to be so...cute?

Once I'd thought of London as cute, it never left my mind. It had been a thought whose presence I'd felt all this time, but it had never surfaced. Not until now. But when it finally came, it blinded me. Its light illuminated me and scorched me. It left me thirsty and suffering.

It left me alone and isolated.

Elle: Are you okay? Where are you?

I sent Elle my location so she could find me on the map. I had no clue where I was. Somewhere north of the strip was all I knew about this place. The road was sloping down to the cliffs and I finally stopped walking.

Elle: What the hell are you doing there? Wait for me. Don't move.

Me: I'll wait. Don't worry.

Elle: I'm on my way.

I left the road behind and stepped over the rocky ground to the edge of one of the cliffs, then sat down. There were flat bits of rock here and there all around me, but I enjoyed sitting on the edge. I enjoyed letting my legs dangle from the cliff and the spray of the ocean's persistent waves reaching my calves.

I can't do this to her, I thought.

Moments passed; minutes, tens of them. They passed in a blur of fear and bitter disappointment. What the fuck had I been thinking? That he would just say, "Oh, sure, Gabriel. Let's make out and have a life together!" I was such an idiot.

Being around London now did this to me. It turned me into a stammering fool. It made me careless. It fogged my brain.

But I wanted it. I wanted every confused moment near him that I could get.

Good job making sure you never get another moment with him again, my voice of reason chimed in.

A car slowed down and a door opened and closed. The car went away, but the footsteps neared me.

"Babe?" she called.

My heart clenched. She shouldn't have called me that. She didn't know.

I turned my head around and looked at her with an already apologetic look on my face.

"What happened?" she asked.

I scrambled around on my knees, then got up and dusted myself off. *Where do I begin?* I stared at her with all the words buzzing around my head. I'd prepared none of them. I'd hardly even thought of it.

Her expression was puzzling. It went from concerned to tired, then back. She extended her hand just as the car that had dropped her off turned around and stopped a couple dozen paces away from us.

I took her hand and followed as she led me toward the car.

"Where are we going?" I asked.

"Anywhere but here," she said and glanced at the rocks behind us. She shuddered. "You don't look too good."

I frowned as I thought about it. Had I given her a reason to worry? Probably. My mind was spinning. It hadn't been my intention.

We got into the car. Elle said something to her chauffeur and we drove off. We eventually reached the location she must have given to him, and we climbed out. Everything was just a still image in my mind. Nothing moved in the flow of time and reality, but in jerky flashes.

"Come on," Elle nudged me toward the bar. "I could use a drink and you look like you really need one."

I followed her reluctantly because she had chosen, somehow, the exact same bar where I'd sat just an hour earlier. Someone else was sitting in London's chair.

We sat down and Elle ordered us drinks, then sighed and shook her head at me. "What's the matter, Gabriel?"

I bit my lip. I couldn't make myself look her in the eyes.

She must have known our relationship hadn't been going well. She must have realized. She hardly ever showed any interest in me, ever. Except, it wasn't her fault at all. Only now did I realize that it might have been me who stalled and evaded. I was the one who had set us up for failure.

"Elle," I whispered.

Her lips pressed together tighter and her eyebrows dragged up.

"Are you happy?" I asked, voice almost a sob, but I fought to keep it more or less normal.

She shrugged. "I'm not unhappy."

"Big difference," I said.

"Is that what this is about?" she asked. "Are you having a panic attack about something?"

I sighed and rubbed my eyes. My head hurt. Every thought that crossed my mind was a razor that slashed. I'd imagined breaking up with her so many times, but never for real. I'd imagined it over some stupid little things, over snide comments and little injustices. It never mattered.

I'd never thought it would come to this. I'd thought we would simply run our course.

Never like this...

"I feel like..." As the words left my lips and our eyes met, I saw him again. I saw him in her as I'd seen him a million times. *It was me all along*, I realized. I had been the reason Elle and I had never had a passionate relationship.

She was my best friend. She was like a sister to me. Just not a girlfriend.

I took a calming breath of air as Elle leaned in. "I feel like I'm trapping us both in this."

She nodded. No emotion flickered in her eyes.

I shook my head. "We hang out. We laugh. We have the best time together, but it doesn't feel like a...relationship."

"It doesn't," she agreed quietly.

I held her gaze. Her words didn't surprise me. I'd felt the coldness for a while, but I hadn't realized I had been the source of it.

It still stung like hell to have to say the words.

"Gabriel," she said softly, a gentle, shy smile touching the corners of her lips. "Let me make this easy for you."

I put my face in my hands and sighed. "Don't." *I don't deserve it.* "Elle, I'm so messed up."

She chuckled. "You're not messed up."

"You've no idea," I said. *Don't be my friend when I'm destroying all our plans. Don't help me.* I got exactly what I deserved; London hated me and Elle would soon enough.

"We were too young when we got together," she said casually. "Besides, long distance was a mistake."

I shook my head. *Stop trying to help me. It'll only hurt more.* "But it's my fault it didn't work. I always thought it was both of us. Sometimes, I thought it was you. But it wasn't. It's all on me, Elle."

She gave a contemptuous snort. "Don't be silly, Gabriel. We're equally to blame and it's not like we spent a lifetime together and grew old with regrets."

I lifted my head and looked at her. The words that were about to shatter the friendship between us teetered at the edge of my tongue.

"You like someone else," she said softly.

I froze.

She nodded. "I mean..." She fixed an imaginary crease on my shirt. "It's not like it doesn't sting my pride, but that's about the end of it."

"I'm sorry," I whispered.

Elle waved her hand in dismissal. "Don't worry about my pride." She bit her lip and looked away. Was she about to tear up? I couldn't take it. But she closed her eyes slowly and I felt the crack pass through my chest. "I like someone else, too," she said.

And just like that, something possessive came over me. *My girl*, I thought for a split second. It bruised my pride just like she'd said, but it was faint and far. It wasn't real, except for the moment of realization that I wasn't the only person she had feelings for. It was vanity, pure and simple. And it was gone as soon as it had appeared.

She opened her eyes and nodded. "This changes nothing," she said, lifting her chin. "We've been best friends since we could talk. I don't see why we couldn't stay friends." She gave me a long, hopeful look. Slowly, she took a deep breath of air, licked her lips, and said the words, "I think we should break up."

Simultaneously, I said, "It's London."

Silence fell between us for a long moment. "What?"

My lip trembled as I tried to force the words out again. "I have a crush on him, Elle."

She blinked and stared at me, expressionless.

"Elle, I'm so fucking sorry. I don't know what's happening to me." I ran my hands through my hair, then folded them over my lips and looked away from her. And still, the fucker was on my mind.

First came a sniff; then came a chuckle. By the time I frowned and looked at Elle, her slender shoulders were shaking with laughter. "I'm sorry," she squealed. "I don't mean to... It's not funny..." She laughed harder to my horror, then finally pulled herself together and took a sip of her drink.

"Why are you laughing? You should...hate me." My frown deepened.

Elle snorted, a final bubble of laughter escaping her. "Does he know?"

It hurt to even mention this. Not only had I thrown him off as far as I could, but I was embarrassed after getting shot down. I nodded.

"Did he tell you about his doodles? I bet he didn't," she shook her head just as I did. "I don't think he knows I know. He always thought he was so sneaky and clever. Hiding them under his mattress as if that wasn't the first place I snooped around." She put a hand on her head. "I swear, I was a terrible sister, but I've changed." She laughed at that.

"What doodles?" I asked.

There was a genuine smile on her face when her gaze met mine. "Of you two. He's a shit artist, but the boy tried. The only way I knew it was you was the fact you were a head taller and there was a capital *G* above your head. But he used to draw you two all the damn time."

My heartbeat quickened and my breaths grew shallow. London had been sketching us together? "When... When was this?"

"Pfft. Years ago."

The boy that had gone away from us had had a crush on me. And I hadn't noticed.

"You're not...angry? You don't hate me?" I narrowed my eyes as if it would help me read the crease on her forehead. But it was genuine surprise at my question, nothing more. "How did we get here, Elle?" I asked, tired and confused.

She shrugged. Her shoulders moved so smoothly that I instantly pictured London. "We were kids, Gabriel. And I feel like our parents sort of expected us to get together and we just did. No offense, but I was never really smitten by you."

I snorted. "None taken."

"I liked you. I love you. It's just not what it's supposed to be, right? Besides, I knew London had a crush on you at some point so I never really gave us a chance, either." She lifted her glass. "To best friends forever, Gabriel."

I chuckled softly and raised my glass. "To you."

"You know I love you like a brother," she said.

I shook my head. "That's why you should be angry with me, Elle."

"Just drop it," she said after taking a sip of her drink. "We got together for all the wrong reasons, but at least we can break up for the right ones. We like other people; we never committed to each other; nothing changes." She folded her hands on the table. "So..." Silence. "Are you two...?"

I shook my head violently. "No way. No. Nothing happened. We, uh... We didn't do anything. And nothing will. He hates my guts now. It's just this..." I touched my chest, right where my heart was. "This new feeling, nothing more." It was too weird to talk about this to Elle. But Elle was the only person I could ever talk to without any fear. "He sort of threatened to tell you if I didn't." I sighed. "I was gonna tell you first, but we were out and I just... I don't know." I covered my face again and groaned. "I let it slip. Stupid. I don't even know..."

"What don't you know?" she asked.

"I don't know what I am," I said and let my hands drop into my lap. "I was attracted to you, early on, but it never went anywhere. I feel like it was too weird for us to, um, do that stuff. I mean, we used to ride sticks for horses together. You don't just forget that and get down to sex, right?"

She laughed out loud. "Yep. That's the part that bothered me, too."

"Did we really just get together because we were expected to?" I asked. For a moment, it felt like I was talking to *my Elle*. This was the girl I loved and knew. It just wasn't the girl I was attracted to. This was my best friend.

She gave a thoughtful nod. "I'm pretty sure that's why."

I sighed. "I've got stuff to work through, now."

Her brow creased again. "Just remember, you don't need a label to be the best guy I know. Straight, gay, furry... Nobody cares."

Is that actually the case? I wondered.

"Just be yourself."

I sniffed. I wasn't sure if I wanted to laugh or cry. If I cried, I didn't know if they would be tears of joy or sorrow. "And the guy you like?" I asked. "I bet he won't be happy if you stay friends with your ex."

She laughed. "If he minds it, he knows where to stick it," she said, but quickly shook her head. "But I don't think he would mind."

"Are you two...?" I echoed her question.

"No," she shook her head fast. "It's just the way he looks at me and I at him. We didn't do anything, but something... I don't know. Something's there."

"He's the luckiest guy in the world," I said and winced at the cheesiness of those words. But I meant every one of them. Whoever Elle loved would be one lucky guy.

She snorted with the unique Reynolds sarcasm that was so like London's. "Yes, I'm a charm."

My heart twisted at the thought of London, but I pushed him out of my head. It was over. It was done.

I yawned and Elle finished her drink, then slapped her hands. "Honestly, I thought something bad had happened."

I frowned. "This isn't bad enough for you?"

We both laughed. "I feel good about this. I feel like we needed a kick to get us to our senses. Sometimes, I thought we'd stay together forever just because neither wanted to start the conversation."

"I was so scared I was going to break your heart, Elle," I said.

She cackled. "Rein in that ego."

And sure enough, nothing else she could have said would have made me feel better than this. We laughed together, ordered another round, and lost ourselves in endless talk of our past.

For the first time in two years, I was talking to the Elle I loved the most. I was talking to my friend. Nothing was in the way. No relationship etiquette that I'd somehow adopted barred me from opening up to her. Oddly enough, we were much more honest tonight than at any point in the last two years.

And the more I thought about it, the more I came to realize she was right. My dad had mentioned Elle in passing so many times, always as 'that nice girl' that was perfect for me. He'd groomed me, perhaps unintentionally, to date her. Mom, too, while she was still around, had a few passing comments, but never as much as Dad. She had found it harder and harder to conform to his rigid rules as the years had gone by and finally snapped one day and left.

We'd stayed in touch, though. I'd forgiven her after a long while. The reason she had left me with Dad instead of taking me with her was purely to ensure a better life, no matter how faulty her logic had been. *He's got money*, she had thought. *He'll take care of my baby boy.*

My resentment toward Dad uncoiled slowly, carefully, in my guts. He would cry and shout and shake his fists at God for making his son gay — if that was even what I was — if only he knew. And my resentment toward Mom came again in traces. Had she only taken me with her, maybe I would have known what family meant.

Either way I sliced it, my future was bleak.

CHAPTER SIX

The Only Way Is Forward

———ele———

I THREW MY BACKPACK on top of a stone table on campus. The sun scorched the earth and I cowered in the shade of an old pine. The benches were mostly empty when I unwrapped my lukewarm sandwich and reluctantly bit into it.

I pulled out a book from my backpack and stared at the cover. *Micro To Macro: Economics Explained*. And just like with the previous books, looking at it pulled an image of Gabriel from the most suppressed repository of my memories.

I barely stifled my growl, tucked two fingers under the knot of my tie, and pulled it loose. Then, I undid the top button of my plain, white shirt, and ignored the book. It would help me pass, but every word of it would hurt like hell.

The son of a bitch was gay or bi or bi-curious and he decided to just come out and say it. *Selfish asshole*, I thought to myself, immediately feeling guilty about that thought. I was fucking in love with him...

I looked up as if something invisible guided me to do so. Across campus, wearing big, black sunglasses, walked Elle, and she was coming my way. *Great. More guilt*, I thought.

Would I tell her? Would I be the asshole who outed him? I couldn't do that. But I couldn't let her date him if he was pulling her leg like this.

"What's up?" Elle asked shortly as soon as she got close to me. She sat on the bench on the other side of the table.

"You came all the way from Foothill to ask that?" I raised an eyebrow.

"No. I had Bradley drive me all the way from Foothill to tell you to quit that brooding brat persona you've created." She lifted her glasses to the top of her head and angry sparks burst out of her eyes.

"What the hell did I do now?" I asked and tore another chunk off my sandwich.

"Let's see. You haven't answered a single one of the twenty-plus calls yesterday; you left all my messages on 'read'; you called Gabriel a lying piece of shit when he came out to you. Am I missing anything?" She cocked her head.

I choked on the dry bit of sandwich and widened my eyes. "I didn't say 'shit,'" I said over a mouthful. "Also, um... What the fuck?"

"Yeah. What the fuck? He didn't deserve that, London." She gave a tired sigh and moved a lock of hair that a gentle breeze brought over her face.

"So, he told you?" I finally swallowed that piece of sandwich and wrapped the rest, then shoved it into my backpack.

"Because you blackmailed him," Elle pointed out.

"*Your boyfriend* is bi-curious. How am I the ass-hole here?" I protested, ever so slightly annoyed.

She shook her head. "You're not an asshole, London. You're just doing a really good impression of one. And I'm here to tell you to drop the act."

"What act? For fuck's sake, Elle. If there's anyone you should be fighting with, it's him." I searched for my bottle of water in the backpack but couldn't find it. I must have left it in the amphitheater.

"Don't pretend you're not in love with him," she said.

Her words cut right through my chest and my mouth went drier. "I don't even like him," I blurted.

"Liar."

"What do you want from me?" I demanded.

Silence lingered between us for a few moments and Elle slouched a little, her facial muscles relaxing. "I don't want to fight, but you're so fucking annoying when you lie."

I threw my hands in the air. "I did nothing wrong. He came to me. I didn't ask him to tutor me; I didn't ask him to tell me all that bullshit. I was perfectly happy before all this." *Liar*, I heard myself shout internally.

Elle shook her head in an over-the-top show of disappointment. "If you think I can't feel your heart fidgeting when he's around, you really are as dumb as you pretend to be."

My throat closed. "Elle," I whispered. "I would never..." *...betray you like this. I would never lay a finger on him. I would rather rip my heart out than take him from you. You have to know that. If I could choose to never feel anything at all just so I don't feel this way for him, I would.*

"Why not?" she asked softly. "Is it so terrible that he dated me first?"

I frowned. "What? No. That's not..." But I couldn't speak. My eyes itched and stung and I really fucking needed a glass of water.

"What is it, then? Because I don't get you." She turned completely soft and it threatened to make me cry. I honestly preferred her anger.

"What happened between you two?" I asked. It was the most I could say.

Of all the things I expected her to do, Elle laughed. She fucking laughed like this was no big deal. "We broke up. Finally, I might add."

I frowned in return. Was I supposed to say I was sorry? Was I supposed to comfort her? Because she sure as hell didn't look in need of any comfort.

"London, it was a childhood relationship. It was never going to last." She gazed at me as if waiting for an answer.

I bit my tongue to draw my brain's attention elsewhere. Otherwise, I would soon fall apart. My eyebrows twitched, my lips trembled, my fingers shook. I held my breath.

"We're both better off as friends." She blew out a breath of air. "He was afraid of hurting me and I felt the same. I figured we'd either be codependent forever or let it die quietly." She waited a little more, but I was still holding my breath. I didn't dare move a muscle, else the facade would finally crack. "I know you had a crush on him before and I am as sure as hell that you still have it now."

My heart twisted with the question that emerged from the depths of my soul and I fought to keep my stare cold and emotionless. "If you knew, then why did you get together with him?" If only I could run away from her in this moment. If only I could hide somewhere and let all the tears out. Maybe then, I could finally breathe free.

She shook her head. "I don't know. I thought I liked him. Now, it seems obvious, but I thought that was what we were meant to do." She leaned in and rested her hands closer to mine on the stone table. "London, it was a mistake. We were both young and confused. Hell, he barely knows who he is now."

I pressed my lips tightly and gazed at her for a long while. "He'll have to find out on his own."

"Do what you will," she said. "But I need you to know that it doesn't bother me. If you want, give him a chance. If you don't, just put him down gently. Don't judge him, little bro."

For the first time in days, I chuckled. "Two minutes," I whispered.

"Yet infinitely wiser," she said of herself.

I looked at the few inches of the table between our hands. I looked there for what seemed like forever. My chest was barely moving as I took short breaths and brought my pulse down. "Gabriel is the only crush I've ever had," I admitted, using his name for the first time.

"I know that, pumpkin," she said.

I snorted. "Never call me that again."

"You'll understand when you're older," she said just as softly. I wondered if she'd ever stop with these corny jokes. But for once, they brightened my mood. "He did a really brave thing, London. It's none of my business what happens next, but be careful. You should know better than anyone that it's not an easy thing to come to terms with."

Great, I had one more reason to feel terrible and want to cry. Poor Gabriel... Lost little boy...

"And you're saying," I began slowly, "that it would be just the most normal thing in the world if I got together with your boyfriend." I snorted. "Which I don't mean to, by the way." *I'm pretty sure I burned that bridge yesterday.*

"Why wouldn't it be? It's not like you guys were fucking around behind my back. And it's not like I'm suffering without him." She shook her head in dismissal. "Our days were always numbered."

"Oh, I dunno, maybe because you slept with him and what if I do, too?" *Holy shit, stop thinking about sleeping with Gabriel.*

"When did it ever bother you who your flings slept with in the past?" Elle asked. She had a coy smile on her face.

I cleared my throat to prevent myself from choking to death. "Maybe when the fling in question slept with my twin sister for two years." I shuddered.

"First of all, so what? Don't be a child. Second, it wasn't for two years, if you must know. We slept together a couple of times early on and that was it." She pursed her lips and held her chin high.

I couldn't believe the words she was saying. Had they really not done it in so long? "It still doesn't change anything. What if... What if I think of you?" I nearly gagged.

She snorted. "Then you are as dumb as you're pretending to be."

Silence fell between us and I thought about everything. I was far from having any sort of answer. Besides, it was all speculation, anyway.

"You know you're an impossible big sister, right?" I asked with a smile.

"I've been told I'm the best," she said and flicked her hair theatrically.

"By the mirror? You know that's you on the other side?"

She smiled and observed me for a short while. "My job here is done, I think."

I snorted. It was nowhere near done. Only now did I come to the real problem of it all. But she couldn't help me with that.

Elle pushed her hands a little forward and they covered mine. "Leave the broody brat behind, little bro."

"I'll try," I said. It was the closest to a promise I dared to go.

I hated this wrapping paper. It had teddy bears all over a beige background. It looked like I was going to a baby shower.

Panic struck me and I wanted to change it to something cooler, but I'd already knocked on his door and the movement on the other side was audible.

The door flew open and Gabriel's jaw dropped. He widened his eyes and raised his eyebrows. "London?" His voice was thin and high-pitched.

"That'd be me," I said, voice strangled. I thrust the wrapped gift forward. "Sorry about the wrapping paper. It sucks."

He carefully took the rectangular package from me. Did I intimidate him? God, I hoped not. He turned it around and frowned, then lifted his gaze to meet mine. "What are you doing here?"

I mulled on my words and looked down, then up at his green-brown eyes. "I came to apologize for the way I reacted."

Gabriel stood at the door for a few moments longer, unsure of what to do. Abruptly, he moved to a side and gestured with his head for me to enter. "Come on, then."

I walked in as fear rose in my stomach. What was I supposed to expect from this? It wasn't like the novels I had stashed under my bed had made it out to be.

Gabriel closed the door of his room and I glanced around. I'd never actually been inside his room. There was a kick-ass TV mounted onto one wall with a gaming station on the small shelf underneath it. The two desks were littered with notebooks and textbooks and countless pens. The beds were tidy, though. And so were the chairs, unlike in my room.

I took a deep breath of air. Why was this so hard? "I'm sorry I made you tell Elle."

"She had every right to know," Gabriel said.

"No. I'm sorry about *making* you tell her. I shouldn't have done that."

Gabriel nodded. He was way more awkward now than any time I'd seen him playing football on the field, which he casually did, or volleyball at the beach. He was way more shy and that was my fault.

"I'm also sorry about the things I said," I added.

He shrugged. "You weren't wrong."

"Oh, I was. I was wrong to react the way I did. Nobody should come out to that," I said, guilt twisting my insides. I wiped my hands against my knee-length shorts and turned around to face the window. "You did come out to me, right? I mean, that's what you were going to say."

Gabriel blew out a tired breath of air. "I don't know, London. Maybe. Is it coming out if I don't even know what I am?"

I shrugged and turned back to face him. "Does it matter, though?"

"I don't know. Does it?" He turned the rectangular gift in his hands.

"I don't know," I said. "I guess, you're the only one who should know."

He let out a soft chuckle. "I'm used to a very organized universe, you see. Equations come easy to me because there's nothing gray about them. They either fit or don't."

"Sexuality's nothing like that," I said. "The amount of times I saw an attractive girl and thought I was maybe bi is ridiculous."

"Are you?"

"No." I smiled at him. "But that's not the point. The point is, nobody's alike. We all have things that do it for us. Yours seems to be Elle's twin brother." I barked out a laugh, not quite believing the words I'd said.

Gabriel was attracted to me. To *me*. I couldn't accept that as reality. The thought had lived in my imagination for much too long. Yet it sparked the oddest sensation in my stomach.

"And only Elle's twin brother," he said softly, almost fearfully. "I've been beating my head for days and there's nobody else that does this to me. Nobody makes me stammer and fidget like this. Nobody thrills me like this either."

My throat seized and I felt the heat rise to my cheeks. Was he really saying this? Had I smacked my head against a road sign and woken up in an alternate reality?

"Is it true you used to draw us?" he asked.

I let out a brief, airy laugh. "I don't know what you dorks like these days, so I winged it. Open the gift."

He chuckled at that. He'd been around a Reynolds for long enough to know we were perfectly incapable of too many serious thoughts.

He tore the paper off and revealed the top gift of the two. It was the newest *Jedi* game. "Wow," he said, eyebrows rising, brow creasing.

"I don't know if you like *Star Trek*. But if I had to guess..."

He shot me a look. "*Now* you have a reason to apologize."

"What?"

"It's *Star Wars*," he said.

I frowned. "I thought they were the same."

"You're on thin ice," Gabriel said and I finally cracked a smile.

"I'm just messing with you," I said. "Look at the other thing."

Gabriel placed the game on his desk and tore the rest of the wrapping paper. He let the bits fall onto the floor and turned an aged notebook in his hands. Some pages were filled with silly little things I'd doodled for practice. But most of them were pages nobody had ever seen.

Except, this fucker apparently knew about my sketches. If I had to guess, Elle had touched my stuff a decade ago and she was in for some scolding.

Gabriel opened the notebook and found the first of the sketches. Two boys, drawn from behind, walking up a hill, and a Siberian Husky trotting between them. One was a head taller and they both had messy hair.

He put a hand on his mouth, eyes teary, and shook his head. "London, this is from years ago."

"You're the reason I found out I'm gay," I admitted, my voice breathy and quiet.

"I never knew," he said.

"When you're afraid to admit something like this, you learn how to lie." I watched him for a little while in total silence.

He glanced at the drawings through my notebook. Every single one of them had two boys and a pup. "You never had a dog," Gabriel said, his voice a little shaky.

"I never had you either," I said. "These were my wish fulfillments and daydreams."

He looked up from the notebook and met my gaze. "I... I don't know what to do."

I shrugged and turned away from him again. "Whatever you want," I said simply.

"Whatever?"

"Yeah."

I was just about to turn back when his hand touched my shoulder and tugged me. I found myself face to face with the boy of my dreams, his eyes shining with unshed tears, lips parting in a mixture of fear and anticipation.

I knew, in my heart of hearts, he was about to do this, but not a single cell in my body was ready. I wanted it more than I wanted to breathe. I wanted it more than I wanted to see another sunset.

Sucking in a quick breath of air, I surrendered myself to his will.

First, I felt the heat of his breath on my lips. But I hardly had enough time to process it. His proximity brought all my senses to high alert. It raised my pulse and made my brain spin.

But even that faded away in an instant because his lips grazed against mine. It was only a brush, a gentle touch, and it disappeared into nothingness a flicker later.

Did he regret it? Did he change his mind? The question popped in my head faster than I could open my eyes to see for myself. But before I did, the entire world collapsed on itself and every atom in the creation disappeared. The only thing that remained, standing like a monument to the universe, was the ferocious touch of his lips against mine.

He pressed harder against me, squeezing a moan out of my chest. It was a wonder I didn't faint in this very moment when all my dreams came true.

The softness of his lips was overshadowed by the searing intensity of his kiss.

Buds bloomed and earth gave life to fresh grass and my entire soul began to shine. His lips moved across mine as he shifted his head.

Gabriel was a damn good kisser. He was so good, in fact, that the room began to spin.

And then, he pulled his head back and sucked in a quick breath of air. "Was that...?"

"Perfect? Yeah." My breaths were shallow and my body was still tingling. My pants were tight and my cock was about to explode. But to hell with it all, my heart was full.

CHAPTER SEVEN

Dare To Touch

——eee——

MY HEART WAS THUMPING its steady way out of my chest. Thrills were soon replaced by chills as I gazed into deep brown eyes that were identical to the eyes I'd looked into for years.

This is wrong, my voice echoed through my skull. But it wasn't. It lifted me from the floor and made me float. It soothed the fears and pains. It was more than just a kiss.

"Do it again," London whispered, eyes like pools of hope; lips like a promise of the sweetest banquet.

Tha-thump, tha-thump, tha-thump.

I held my breath and rested my hand on the back of his head, fingers twining with his straight brunette locks. Somehow, the fear that crawled into my heart made this moment even more exciting. Grazing his lips with mine, then touching them firmly, then parting them to allow him to explore my mouth with his tongue tasted like something forbidden.

I silenced the voices that warned me about my dad, about Elle, about everyone in the world. I silenced the questions about my sexuality because I was way out of my depth here. All my thoughts converged around London.

His slender fingers nearly dug into my chest. A whimper burst out of his lips and I inhaled it.

London's other hand touched the side of my waist and tugged me into him. Our bodies bumped and London thrust his hips forward, sending my heart into a meltdown. *He really is nine inches long*, I thought, panic striking me to my marrow. There was no mistaking the sudden firmness in his pants, the bulge that rubbed hard against me. But there was no mistaking mine, either. He had to be aware.

This though, too, made my palms slick with perspiration. He was aware of my hard cock; it was probably on his mind; he was probably picturing it. My chest grew tight and I slipped my tongue between his red lips as if to distract myself. Exploring his mouth — *his*, not *hers*, for the first time in my life — was deliciously easy, yet my fears lurked from the dark corners of my subconsciousness.

London's hand trailed my waist and felt my abs, then dipped lower. Though he'd done it slowly and with more care than I would have expected, the touch of his fingers against my raging erection jerked my feet back. "Wait," I gasped. "Wait."

"What is it?" he asked and blinked at me as I turned my gaze away.

My hand rose to the back of my neck. "It's just... I..."

"Too soon," London said. "That's okay. I'm sorry."

"Don't be," I blurted and raised my gaze to meet his warm, brown eyes. "*I'm* sorry."

The painfully apologetic expression on his face melted away. The teeth biting his lip relaxed and he lifted one corner into a half-smile. "Don't apologize. It's on me. I rushed it."

"I guess I'll get used to...um...," I stammered.

"My hand on your dick?" London asked with an abundance of humor in his voice.

"That. Yes." I laughed with him.

London took my hand in both of his, then pulled me around to my bed. "Let's just sit a little."

"We can kiss more," I said, heat creeping up my neck.

London chuckled as we dropped onto the bed and curled our legs under our asses. "There's nothing I'd rather do, but, uh..." his cheeks turned rosy again. "If we do, my dick might shatter."

We shared a laugh and I glanced down. Even sitting like this, torso leaning forward, I could see the sharp, thick outline of his majestic length. The duality of my soul and heart, and let's face it, also my dick, was killing me. I wanted nothing more than to tear his clothes off his body and see him fully, but even thinking it made me want to crawl into my shell.

"Show me that *Jedi* crap I got you," he said instead. "That should do it."

I snorted. "For you, maybe."

"I should have known it'd be an aphrodisiac for a dork like you," he said, eyebrows flat, cheeky grin emerging.

"Like you didn't know what you were doing," I teased back and hopped onto my feet. My dick was still hard as fuck and I slowed down my movements and turned away from London. I didn't know why I was embarrassed of my hard-on, but I was. Of all the people who would ever judge me for it, London was nowhere near that list. I told myself it was simply the newness of the sensation that raised all these questions, but I feared, deep down, that there was more to it.

He'll disinherit me the moment he finds out. Say your farewells to the gaming console and surround sound system. Say goodbye to your nice clothes and going out. And say 'hello, nice to meet you,' to working your ass off as a bag boy in a grocery store.

I inserted the disc into the gaming console and pushed the thoughts of my dad all the way out of my head. It was *Jedi* time with London. Hanging out with him like this, intimately yet casually, hadn't been a dream I'd had for long, but it was all I could ever wish for.

London played it cool, but I could see his insecurity in the lines on the outside corners of his eyes. I could see it in the way he licked his lips quickly. I could see it in the way his Adam's apple rose and fell as he swallowed.

I sat back next to him and lifted my joystick, but completely forgot about the game the moment my gaze met his smooth cheek. "What made you come here?" I asked abruptly.

London smiled to himself as he looked down. The silence was vastly different from the one we'd had stewing between us mere days earlier. This one was comfortable and soothing. London was thinking. Then, he lifted his head. "When I was eleven, you grinned at me like you had a million times before. But that time was so playful that it sucked the last atom of oxygen out of my chest."

My heart flickered with sadness. He'd been such a cute boy, identical to Elle. Everyone had always known they would grow up to be excruciatingly beautiful. I'd known it. To think that he had spent nearly a decade pining after *me*, it nearly tore my chest open.

I had always known London was on another level. He was quirky and gorgeous, sarcastic yet profound. He was so fucking special that it had blinded me. I'd known, all this time, that he was unique. Only, I'd never understood that it was physical attraction that made me know these things.

London shrugged. "I thought it'd pass, to be honest. But it never did."

I bit my lip in reply. There were no words I could string together to say anything remotely worthy of his feelings.

"See, nothing changed. Not ever. So, when Elle stormed across campus today and called my bluff, the only place I wanted to go was here." He looked at the space between us.

"Elle did that?" I whispered.

London nodded, not looking up. "I never would've had the guts to do anything if she didn't. Even though I wanted to every day since the day you gave me that grin."

I swallowed, more sure about this than about anything in my entire life so far, I waited for London to lift his gaze. The moment he did so, with that same half-smile stuck on his face, I dropped the joystick to one side and virtually rolled onto him.

Ten lost years of unrequited pining to be repaid did not seem like a daunting task when the payment was in his searing kisses.

London fell back after the impact and I followed, not allowing our bodies to separate for even a millisecond. I didn't know where I was going with this. I was led by instinct, by a relentless urge to hold him, and by a possessive feeling that he would only ever be mine. Right now, I would surrender my body and soul to him if he would do the same.

Our lips pressed together tightly for a brief moment.

London pulled back and blinked at me in surprise, but my intentions clicked in his brain and his eyes sparked with the neediness that might as well have been a reflection of my own. His elbows were poking into the mattress, his upper back was still above the bed. London pushed himself a few inches higher, parted his honeyed lips, and kissed me back with all the heat of a newborn star.

Only the dim yellow lamplight and the blue TV screen from across the room lit his handsome features, casting stark shadows on the other side of his face when I pulled back to look at him. The sight of his tongue flicking out to lick his lips, bruised from my hungry kisses, made my heart trip.

I leaned in again and kissed him harder. He never made a sound of protest, though I knew he would, should he want to. Nobody strong-armed London into anything he didn't want to do. It was a miracle Elle even had to push him here, where he already wanted to go.

I could have fallen to my knees and kissed Elle's feet for sending London to me. I would, the very next time I had a chance.

But now, I pressed harder against him. My chest pushed into his and my crotch, cock throbbing, ground against his. London whimpered and pulled his head back with a pained chuckle. "You're killing me, Gabriel."

"I'll make it worth your while," I promised.

"It's not too soon?" he asked, following it with a sexy lip-bite that made me forget the question.

I shook my head. "I'll trust your instincts."

"I've had a decade of imagining this," London said soothingly. It was all the encouragement I needed.

My arm curled around his back and London dropped from the half-lifted position he was in. I tumbled onto him, all the way up his length, and kissed his lips, his cheeks, and his chin that had a slight shadow of a trimmed beard. His chin and mustache were the only spots with a hint of hair and they framed his long face beautifully.

I kissed his jawline and reached the bottom edge of his ear, then sank my teeth into its softness.

London bubbled with laughter and pushed my chest, so I pulled back, met his hungry gaze, and dove back in. My lips pressed against his neck, the sharp cologne he wore entered my nostrils. The unmistakably male scent did things to me that were so much more wild compared to the sweetest, more subtle scent I'd known so far. My cock throbbed hard and I wanted to whimper and moan into London's neck, but I swallowed the sounds and kissed him passionately. I kissed him harder, sucked his tender skin between my lips, and marked him as mine.

He would wear this mark with pride. And I would wear any mark he left on me just the same.

Would you, though? A voice asked. *Would you also tell people who left that mark on you?*

I barked internally at myself to shut the hell up. No question mattered here and now. I wouldn't let them matter. Not tonight.

When I dared slide my hand under London's T-shirt, feeling his smooth, taut skin covered with a thin layer of perspiration drove me wilder yet. I rubbed his firm abs, feeling them tense under my fingertips. I dragged my hand higher and higher still, only to feel a boy's flat, chiseled chest. Each new inch I felt with my hand made my cock ache more. Each sigh that left his sweet lips traversed through me like an earthquake's tremendous vibration.

To my cloudy, lust-hazed mind, it seemed like London either didn't know what to do with either of us, or he didn't dare push me too far. Yet I couldn't let go of his smooth chest. I couldn't resist pinching his nipple with my thumb and index finger. I couldn't stop sucking on his neck and making him wiggle from tickling.

Finally, I pulled my hand out from under his T-shirt and found his. I looked into his eyes and helped his hand to my waist, then dragged it lower to my ass. "Don't worry. I won't panic."

He smiled at me. "What are your boundaries?" he asked.

"I don't have the slightest idea," I said.

He sniffed a chuckle and shook his head. "Then I have to worry."

"Nah." I shook my head to emphasize it. "You only need to help me find them."

London squeezed my ass abruptly and the sensation shot right into my dick, kicking the air out of my lungs while it was at it.

London raised his head and smacked his lips against mine, bit the bottom one, and tugged his head back while clenching his teeth around my flesh. I followed, letting out a suppressed growl, yet soaring with the feeling. This guy, who was half a foot shorter and a good thirty, forty pounds lighter than me, could do whatever the hell he wanted with me and I wouldn't mind. This beautiful guy, who not only would lose the match, but also his arm in an arm-wrestling contest against me, was welcome to toy with me, put me in my place, and own my body to do with whatever pleased him.

My balls tightened as soon as I pictured him towering above me. My dick throbbed and I feared I would come from my thoughts alone. It helped me none when London thrust his hips up and ground his crotch against mine as he let go of my lip.

I glanced at the narrow space between us where his shorts bulged immensely. "Uh... Are you really nine inches?" I whispered, his words from a few days earlier echoing in my mind. I grinned at the silliness of the question.

London's eyebrows danced. "Only one way to find out, soldier."

I snorted at the last word, but didn't hesitate to lift my torso and cross my arms around my waist. I took the corners of my T-shirt firmly in both my hands and tore the thing over my head. My muscles tensed in a show of pride and vanity. They tensed even more so when London, still on his back, put a hand on the middle of my chest.

I was kneeling between his legs as he dragged his hand slowly down my rigid abs.

"Holy fuck, Gabriel," he whispered as if awestruck. "You've no idea how many times I've pictured this."

"Yeah?" It was a whispered purr.

"Hell yeah," he said as he bent his other arm, dug his elbow into the mattress, and lifted his torso. "Just... Give me a moment."

A grin began to emerge, tugging on the strings in my facial muscles more and more as London felt my body and absorbed the moment. That was what he was doing; remembering this.

I, too, forced this moment straight to my long-term memory. It wasn't allowed to ever fade or crack. I needed it intact forever.

London moved his hand away from my chest and placed it in front of his face, then clicked an invisible camera for a mental photo. By far, he was the cutest creature on this planet, now more than ever.

In an instant, the invisible camera was gone, and London was rising up and sliding his T-shirt over his head. He threw it on the floor and dropped back, arms falling above his head, half-dangling from the bottom edge of the bed.

I tenderly touched the sides of his ribcage and dragged my hands down to his narrow waist. Every line of his torso was sharp, every muscle lean, every inch smooth and lightly tanned from a shirtless summer.

He shuddered at my touch, but didn't protest. Instead, his hands came down onto mine and he navigated them to the middle of his lower abdomen. "If you're still curious," he said quizzically.

"I'm dying to know," I said.

He simply smiled and removed his hands from mine.

I tucked my fingers abruptly inside his shorts and waited, but no warning or protest came. London watched me intently, lust unraveling in his eyes, burning everything in its path.

When I began to pull his shorts down, I could have sworn my heartbeat was visible in my throat. It pounded in my head. The murmurous flow of my blood filled my ears.

Down, down, down his shorts dragged over his big cock that was packed tightly in his black briefs dotted with plain red crosses. The sinfulness of his print exhilarated me nearly as much as the act of undressing him.

I choked on the abundance of oxygen that flooded into my lungs when London's cock throbbed and the motion showed.

"You really are killing me," he said, voice somehow squeaky and airy at once.

I jerked his shorts down his pretty smooth upper legs, then further down, where hair grew somewhat thicker. I finally tugged them over his rising feet and threw them away, only to let my hands snatch his tight briefs under the small of his back.

London purred as he lifted his hips and I pulled his underwear over his small, yet perfectly round ass. It shouldn't have surprised me to see there was no tan line on his hips as much as it did. Of course he picked the beaches where he could tan evenly. But I forgot all about his tan the moment the front side of the waistband pulled his cock down and revealed a short trimmed patch of black hair.

I saw myself leaning in before I realized I'd done it. My lips touched the skin under his belly button and traced the middle until I felt the short, coarse hair under them. Fear and thrills, shame and excitement, they all mixed into a seductive cocktail I could sip for the rest of my life.

My hands moved over his bare ass cheeks and London moaned. I vaguely noticed him grabbing the blanket on both sides and closing his fists tightly around them. My hands circled his narrow waist and found the pesky briefs that separated me from what I wanted the most.

Time stopped altogether when my fingers reached inside the waistband. Maybe, for an instant, I even felt the shaft of his cock. It didn't matter because I lifted the waistband over his solid nine inches of girth with a precum slicked head, and his cock literally jumped and fell straight over his lower abdomen. A faint trace of musk mixed with a skin lotion sent water to my mouth and I had to fight not to drool all over him.

"Fuck," I murmured. "It was smaller in my head."

"And for how long has my cock been in your head?" London teased.

It took me a moment to compose myself. I licked my lips and smiled to myself. "Long enough."

I made a quick job of pulling London's sinful briefs all the way down his lean, muscular legs, and wrapped them into my fist, reluctant to let go. The only reason I did finally throw them away, was the fact that this naked beauty still lay in front of me, waiting. His cock stiffened as soon as I reached for my denim shorts to undo the top button and unzip the rest. It stayed upright as I got off the bed and stepped out of my shorts.

I stood still, chest heaving, in nothing but a pair of dark blue boxer-briefs. My dick was pitching a tight tent off my left hip and London scanned my entire body, then licked his lips.

"Take them off," he whispered.

I did so silently, not even flinching. Later, my heartbeat would probably double its speed, when I remember that I'd been naked and horny next to an equally naked and horny guy — London, no less — but now, I let my underwear drop, stepped out of them, and watched his triangular torso rise and fall with steady breaths.

"You're so fucking beautiful," I said as I returned to the bed, kneeling between his spread, bent legs. My gaze followed each cut line of his chest muscles, then his abs, and finally to his massive cock and big, heavy balls, hanging swollen over his taint. Just underneath them, in the shadow, I saw the merest hint of his hole as I rested my hands on his thighs.

"So are you," he said, gaze falling down my big, bulky body, following the thin hairline that led from my belly button to my neatly cropped bush, and then to my equally hard and slick cock.

"What do you want to do?" I asked, feeling stupid all of a sudden for asking.

London gave a lazy smile. "I'll be happy staying like this if that's what floats your boat." Then, he chuckled. "But you should know that I want to do everything there is under the sun."

This raised my pulse and my temperature by a few degrees.

"But... One step at a time," he said softly and pushed himself up on his elbows once again. The tension in his torso was so irresistible that I simply crashed onto him and kissed him for no better reason than wanting to.

He kissed me back as passionately, our lips moving over one another, the tips of our tongues playing with each other. There was one thing on my mind and the more I thought about it, the more I knew I wouldn't let this end before I got it.

I dragged my head down to kiss his bruised neck and leave traces on his skin over his hard chest. He chuckled, but never once pushed me away, as I made my descent to the place where both our pleasure's lay.

Once I was there, I took a slow breath of air. "Tell me if I hurt you," I whispered. His cock throbbed in reply.

"Haven't you noticed? I'm kinda tough." His cheeky smile was all the encouragement I needed.

My gaze dropped from his stunning, chestnut eyes to the tip of his cock and the small smear of precum next to his belly button and I opened my mouth. No thought remained in my mind. Only action.

I wrapped my fingers around the base of his cock and pulled it back just enough to close my lips around the tip. The sensation exploded in my chest, warmth spreading to the ends of my nerves, tingling reaching every cell in my body.

I felt his cock against my tongue and the salty taste of his precum filled my mouth and filled my mind.

Every last shred of me tensed with anticipation. The fear of scraping his cock with my teeth crippled me. I'd been on the receiving end of a few terrible blow jobs before I first got together with my now ex. I knew what a turn off such a thing was.

Folding my lips under my teeth, letting my saliva drip from the corners of my mouth all the way down his cock, I took an inch more of him and realized it was already a mouthful.

But London let out a shuddering breath and cut his voice off. His hand found mine and he lifted it, then placed it on the middle of his chest. "This feels so good," he hissed and I all but lost it. Was it possible? Was he just saying that? Ah, but it didn't matter. If he was just saying it, he cared. If it was really so good, he was pleased. Either way, both of us won.

I stretched my jaw as much as I could, yet somehow, he still filled my mouth. Breathing steady through my nose, I thought I discovered a trick. My fingers squeezed around the lower half of his cock and I jerked him off slowly in the rhythm of my head's motion. Each time I lowered my open mouth along his thickness, I made it a little further.

And he moaned. Quietly, at first, but louder with each passing minute. Had it been minutes? Or seconds? It might as well have been hours for all I knew. My awareness was clouded wherever there was none of his body and soul. He was all I knew.

My dick itched hard, as if from somewhere deep inside. I closed my hands around it and found it wet, a strand of precum leaking down to the blanket beneath us.

I tugged once, twice, and felt my balls tighten and rise. *Oh shit. Not so soon.* But London's increasing moans and sweat breaking over his sexy chest pushed me so fucking close to the edge. He tensed, muscles locking, and quickly pushed my head away.

"Fuuuuuck," he growled as I continued jerking him off. His thick, long dick pulsed in my hand and cum shot out in fucking buckets. Though he had pushed my head away — regrettably, I might add — I was close enough to have the hot whiteness land on my face. The contact, a mere moment, jerked my entire body and I heaved over the edge of my climax. Jerking my dick ruthlessly and in the same rhythm as I kept stroking London through his entire blissful suffering, I cried out and felt the cum shoot from my balls.

"Fuck, Gabriel," London whispered, his voice strained. "That was...so...fucking..."

"Awesome," I finished for him as the earthquake that rocked my body passed.

I stopped stroking us both and felt a bubbling pride rise in me. I'd actually done this to us. I'd made us see stars.

I crawled up, not caring an iota for the mess we'd made. Mess could be cleaned. But I would rather be damned than miss this moment with him. I'd needed him here before, in this exact position, and I finally had him. I collapsed on top of him, arms wrapping around his body tightly.

London played along all too happily. He threw his leg around mine and closed his arms around my upper torso.

"Is this real?" he asked softly, carefully.

"I don't know," I said. "But if we're in a computer simulation, I hope nobody trips over the cord."

"Oddly romantic," London said with a mix of sarcasm and genuine calm.

We stayed like that, silent, holding one another's heated body for ages. Time went by as if independent of us. It felt as if I could open my eyes and see the time pass everywhere around us, just not taking us with it. We were in our own bubble universe, not abiding by the laws of physics and nature.

But we couldn't stay there forever. Not yet, at least.

The end of it came spontaneously. We both somehow relaxed and moved off each other, then off the bed. I walked into the bathroom and brought back a warm, wet cloth to wipe us both clean. After that, we dressed, exchanging a few cheeky glances. The moment his blasphemous underwear covered his cock, I missed his nakedness.

"I wish you'd stay," I said.

"Your roommate's bound to show up at some point," London said, dropping his T-shirt over his perfect body. "Next time, you'll come to my place. I'll send Hudson away and you can stay over."

I scratched the back of my head. "Thanks for...understanding."

"All in good time," he said as he moved slowly away from me and toward the door. There, he spun around, uncertainty filling his handsome face. "Gabriel..."

"Yeah?" I asked and stood a foot away from him.

"It's too late now to ask, but..." He looked down at the small space between us. "Whatever comes next," his eyes met mine again, pleading and somewhat colder, as though he was putting a wall shield up already. "Don't make me just an experiment."

I came up short with words. Instead, I snatched his hip with one hand and his face with the other, then pressed my lips hard against his. This was the first time I kissed him since our orgasms and it tasted just as sweet if not more so. "You're never going to be that," I said afterward, light-headed from the intensity of the kiss.

"Good," he said with a curt nod. "I'll see you tomorrow, huh?"

"You call and I'll be there," I said softly.

His nod was more generous this time, even touched by a smile. And then, he walked out.

I hung at the door as he walked down the hallway and toward the stairs.

Look back, I called with my mind. *One... Two... Three.*

London's head spun and a cheeky grin emerged across his face. It was in this moment that I knew how eleven-year-old London felt all that time ago. The grin was brief, almost too normal to talk about, yet it pulled all the air out of me and left me gasping for more long after he was out of sight.

CHAPTER EIGHT

Book Browsing

———ele———

EVERY LAST BIT OF me buzzed throughout the night.

I showered when I got to my room, put on a pair of boxer-briefs, fired up the air-con in the room, and lay on my back, staring at the ceiling.

When Hudson's footsteps neared our room and the door creaked open, I pretended to be asleep. If he only so much as asked what was up, just casually, a river would break a dam and I would tell him everything.

I wasn't like this all the time. I almost never was. But every trace of Gabriel's kisses and touches still spread shivers over my body.

Hudson was quiet as he entered the bathroom and came back a few minutes later. He dropped his clothes off and lay down, covered himself with the thin blanket, and his breathing changed within minutes. He was fast asleep.

Me? I could barely keep my eyes closed.

I stared at the ceiling again and replayed every moment of my evening with Gabriel. I watched it like it was a film, from the moment I knocked on his door to the moment he knocked the soul out of my body.

I'd been rash to jump into his bed and only after asking not to be his experiment. But whatever way I looked at it, I couldn't find a way to regret it. I couldn't find it in me to worry if he would change his mind. I'd gotten all that I had ever wanted. I'd gotten to live out my wildest fantasies.

There was only one little problem; now, I wanted so much more.

Perhaps I drifted asleep for a short while. I wasn't sure. The only thing I knew was that I blinked and the outside seemed a little lighter. Hudson was still breathing evenly, ten feet away from me, totally unaware that my life was upturned.

As the eastern sky brightened, I slipped out of my bed and walked out of our room. It didn't bother me that I was only covered with a small piece of textile and it wouldn't bother any of my friends and brothers-by-fraternity-tradition. We were a close-knit gang of so-called Fuckboys — *thank you very much, Jayden and Alex* — and we sort of wore that with pride. College was there to make mistakes and I'd made plenty. But the knotting in my guts came from a creeping fear that I had been someone's mistake. Gabriel's.

Cold sweat covered my palms as I headed into our spacious kitchen and began preparing a bowl of cereal. What if he woke up today with regret gripping his heart? He'd promised me I wouldn't only be his experiment, yet neither of us was in any control over our hearts. Mine thumped fearfully in the morning light and the clarity that came with it. Some things simply seemed smarter in the veil of darkness.

I carried my breakfast to the common room and crashed into an armchair, ate, and kept glancing at my phone. Not that he had to text me or anything. But wouldn't it be nice? What I wasn't looking at was the large clock on my screen displaying 5:48 AM.

If I focused, I could still feel his open palm sliding up my torso, his fingers closing around my right nipple, his mouth wrapping around my cock. A stirring passed through me and made my dick ever so slightly harder.

By instinct, I opened my chat with Gabriel. The wasteland that was his social media gave me no clue as to how he felt. Then again, we weren't kids anymore. I wasn't really expecting him to post 'SO EXCITED AFTER TONIGHT' before going to bed with some cryptic emoji.

The messages were more frequent in our recent chat, but they pretty much boiled down to agreeing on the time for tutoring. My heart skipped a beat at that thought. Was he going to tutor me again? Were we going to spend endless, grueling hours beating down the formulas only to get exhausted and devour each other to blow off some steam? My legs pressed together, thighs rubbing, cock aching as it woke up, ready for action.

I slurped my cereal and ignored the alluring call to lock myself in the bathroom and take care of my growing problem. I never noticed the three dancing dots at the bottom of my screen. All I saw was:

Gabriel: *Morning, beautiful.*

Crap. He knows I saw the text.

Gabriel: *That was quick. You reading our texts?*

My heart went into overload and pounded all the way out of my chest. I dropped the bowl onto the small table in front of me and locked my phone, then covered my face.

I grabbed my phone in the next instant and typed back a quick and mysterious 'maybe.'

Gabriel: *LOL sadly we don't have a rich history of messages to reread.*

Me: *Improve it, then :)*

Gabriel: *I just might.*

Me: *I'm also into visual arts.*

All the air left my lungs when the next thing that arrived was a photo of his smiling face from a high angle with his bare, muscled torso within the frame. Down there, black boxer-briefs covered the center of my world.

Me: You're gorgeous, but I'm sure you can do better than that :)

Gabriel: I sure can try.

The next photo, almost identical to the last one, had Gabriel wearing a cheekier smile, and his hand, instead of dangling uselessly by his side, had its thumb hooked inside his underwear. The waistband was pulled low enough to reveal his dark, trimmed bush, and my heart climbed into my throat.

Me: Holy fuck! You really are going to kill me.

Another photo had another inch to show and even the base of his cock was visible and it totally cut off the flow of air into my lungs. Open mouthed, I stared at my screen.

Me: I have to see you.

Gabriel: Where? Your place?

Me: Nah. Hudson's still sleeping.

Gabriel: Library?

Me: On my way.

A moment later, he texted again.

Gabriel: <3 :)

I jumped off the armchair and straightened, then immediately slowed down because my hard-on was fucking painful. Wading toward my room, I dressed lightly. A loose T-shirt with no sleeves and sporty shorts without any buttons or zippers for easy access, in case such was needed, fit me well. In the bathroom, I ran a wet hand through my hair, brushed my teeth, washed my face, and raced out. I was almost skipping in my stride toward the library, then slowed down once I was inside. The whole place was empty this early in the morning, except for one lonely librarian sorting through index cards so fervently that she failed to notice me. Casually, I made my way to the economics and business section in the back and noticed movement behind one of the bookcases.

I elected to turn right and have the bookcase between me and the person that was moving. Then, I pretended to be browsing titles, and pulled out a thick, hardcover textbook printed first in nineteen-thirty-nine as if these PhD sources had any value for me. Between the books, I spotted the green-brown eyes that looked back with lust.

"I didn't know the shrines to boredom were open this early," I said flatly.

"Shrines to boredom, are they?" he asked, voice low and husky. It did unspeakable things to my body and I had only just gotten down.

I gave a fake, uninterested shrug. "I said what I said."

Gabriel grabbed his chest. "You wound me, London."

"Oh?"

"Uh-huh."

I replaced the hardcover textbook and dragged my finger across the books from right to left, walking toward the edge of the bookcase. Gabriel followed on the other side until we were face to face with no books between us.

He extended his hand and I took it gladly. "I'll make it up to you," I said.

The sound he made was nothing short of wheezing.

Gabriel pulled me after him, into the privacy of the bookcases, and I couldn't help myself but smile. "So, you didn't change your mind," I said.

"Changed my mind?" he asked and lifted an eyebrow. Slowly, his hand moved along my arm, all the way to my shoulder. It lingered there for a few good moments, then cupped my cheek. "I'm not turning straight if that's what worries you," he said with a half-smile.

I took half a step toward him and felt the heat of his body.

"And I'm not losing interest as quickly as I found it, either," he said.

My smile stretched further and I tried to bite it back. He didn't need to see me sparkling with emotions.

"Because, if you haven't noticed, I have a bit of an obsessive streak in me," he said, voice dropping lower, vibrating down to my stomach.

I moved my other foot closer to him and our chests touched briefly. His hand was still firmly on my face.

"When I get into something, I rarely leave," he said.

"You mean like *Star Trek*?" I teased in a low voice dripping with my neediness for more than just a touch of his hand.

"Careful, London," he said with a suppressed laugh. His other hand touched my hip and I nearly tumbled into a heap of limbs and soppy feelings.

Instead, I found my inner strength and snatched the sides of his waist, forcing him a step back. He bumped into a bookcase and I pinned him there, my hips pushing into him, my chest pressed against his. "Are you saying you're obsessed with me?" I teased.

"I might be," he said in what sounded like a sort of surrender. It felt like he had just given up all the control. It was like a breaking point where he was more than willing to hand me the reins and I took them with all my strength.

As my crotch pressed harder against his, I found exactly what I'd been looking for. He was rock hard and the impact left him breathless. His face got a touch of pinkness and I finally let my smile show. "You really are obsessed," I whispered, gently moving my hips left and right to tease him.

I pushed myself up on my feet, just a few inches, and pressed my lips hard against his. I could hardly believe that last night hadn't been just a boyish dream. I could hardly believe I was kissing him again.

Gabriel placed his hands on my hips and whimpered from the heat of our kiss. It was low and quiet, but it was definitely there. He sucked in my bottom lip and bit it gently. He should have known I would pay him back. Especially for the three separate hickeys I was wearing on my neck.

I thrust my hips forward, showing neither of us any mercy. He grunted and clutched my hips, forcing me to stay pressed against him.

"I'm so fucking obsessed with you," he murmured in between the kisses.

My heart really was going to explode.

"I can't figure it all out, but I am. It's all about you." He broke the contact between our lips only for long enough to murmur these words and I swooned.

"We don't need to talk about it now," I said with a naughty smirk.

He lifted his eyebrows, but I answered that question before he could ask. My hand moved from his hip and felt his hard cock over his shorts.

Gabriel's ears twitched and his grin was more than radiant. "Are you sure? Here?"

"Why not?" I asked.

He bit his lip in excited anticipation and shrugged. "No reason I can think of right now."

So I kissed him again, harder, until the kiss traveled through his body and made his cock pulse so strong that I felt it through two layers of fabric.

He returned the favor within a few heartbeats. First, he squeezed my ass hard like he was holding on for dear life; then, his hand traveled around my waist and reached for my length.

Picking boxer-briefs was the smartest goddamn decision I had ever made in my entire life. The briefs I'd worn last night had nearly killed me with pressure on my fully hard cock. This way, even though it was tight, at least I had some room to, uh, grow.

My hand dragged up from Gabriel's cock to feel his abs while the other hand undid the top button of his shorts. I unzipped them, then returned my hand to his hip and searched his bubbly ass. Once I felt his abs thoroughly, I let my hand slide inside his underwear.

He never made a sound until now. He moaned into my mouth, then cut the kiss short and buried his face in my neck, not to kiss it or mark it as his, but to stifle his moans.

I closed my hand around his thick cock and almost shivered. I was holding him in my hand after so many nights of imagining it. It felt infinitely better. It felt as though every illusion I had ever had was shattered and the real thing was unimaginably more satisfying.

The flickering of lust rushed through my body as I stroked him. My unsteady, short breaths grew a little louder, so I opted to stop breathing altogether.

That failed once Gabriel got to his senses a little and began nuzzling my neck, his hand slipping inside my underwear.

"You're so fucking big," he whispered into my neck as he gave a lazy tug inside my pants. The second one was not lazy at all. It was a firm, determined stroke that was on a mission. "So fucking big," he whispered again, as if lightheaded. "I can't wait to...ah..." His cock pulsed in my hand. "...take you..." It pulsed again.

But so did mine. I hadn't even pictured it yet. I hadn't even gotten to that fantasy, but the images of sliding between his cheeks, penetrating him from behind, holding his back pressed hard against my chest, made me throb and want to come immediately.

"London," he whispered, breathless. "This is...crazy..."

"Should I stop?" I asked.

"Hell no," he said and thrust his hips shortly, fucking my fist. I stiffened my grip and jacked him faster. "Don't stop," he pleaded in a whisper, followed by a sigh.

His hand traveled up and down the length of my cock, pace and pressure increasing with each stroke.

"It's crazy...how much...I want you to...fuck me," he said and my cock pulsed harder. The orgasm caught me suddenly, totally unprepared. Cum squirted out of my cock almost for as long as last night. The sensation, akin to a rolling thunder or far-out waves reaching the shore, rose through me. My cock twitched on as I plastered my lips hard against him and forced my moans down his throat for silence's sake.

Stroking me still, Gabriel moaned right back into my mouth, and stiffened where he stood. His cock pulsed in my hand violently. His warm wetness spilling into my fist and through my fingers.

We shuddered against one another, holding tight as if not to collapse or let the other one fall. But the buzzing sound of reality reached me soon and I remembered where we were. Pulling myself together, I slipped my messy hand out of his shorts and gave a guileless shrug with a grin.

He did the same.

In the back of the library, a small restroom was stowed away, so we headed over there to wash our hands.

"How about now?" I asked, half-jokingly. "Any regrets?"

"Nope. None at all," he said casually.

"Good," I said, pretty damn pleased. Before we left the restroom, I faced him and planted a gentle kiss on his lips. There wasn't a moment, not a split second, in which he seemed unsure of it. "You're not bi-curious," I whispered reassuringly.

He lifted his eyebrow. "Sure about that already?"

"I think I am," I said. "But you know what?"

"Hm?"

"I don't care what you call it," I said and rested both my hands on his broad, muscled chest. "It doesn't matter to me."

"Thank you," he said, as if not quite sure how to reply.

I didn't need him to reply at all. He just needed to know that I wouldn't pressure him.

"I swear, it's not just a passing fancy," he said slowly, with great care. "I don't know what it is. I might never know." He shrugged. "But it's here to stay, I promise."

Well, if that didn't merit another kiss, nothing ever could.

The boy in me woke up and lived. For one shining moment, it was that summer again, and the boy who fell in love with the shiniest grin in the world knew that, someday, he would be the center of the grinning boy's world. Even if only for a moment.

CHAPTER NINE

World of Our Own

———ℓℓ———

I HEADED DOWN THE hill on foot. My new, black sunglasses, with a tiny golden brand name inscribed, protected me from the piercing brightness of Santa Barbara's early fall sunshine.

The downhill road led straight to the strip along the beach, where I was headed. The entire road was framed by towering palm trees that gave just enough shade to save my pricey shoes from melting on the heated concrete.

After the last lecture of the day, I stopped by my room, made arrangements, and got down to work. On my laptop browser, I had about a quarter million tabs open and you can bet I read everything I could. The study topic of the day: how to bottom?

It had been five days since the heat of the moment in the library when I told him I wanted more. He probably didn't believe me. Not fully. I figured that was the thing with wanting something for half your life; when it happened, it seemed too good to be true. London, even if subtly, seemed to expect everything to blow up at any moment.

And I was damn ready to prove him wrong. I hadn't been joking when I told him it was his job to find my limits. I knew less about myself than I had ever imagined and I needed him to guide me. But he would rather put his hand in fire than tug me where he wasn't sure I wanted to go.

I'd seen him between classes every day of the week. I'd seen him in the library, too, and we had a good reason to exchange pink-cheeked smiles.

But now, when I reached the beach and spotted him sitting in the distance, I had to stop moving and take in the sight of him. He was far from any of the crowds, his back leaning against the rocky cliff. The suit jacket of his uniform doubled as his blanket that he spread out over the sand and his shoes were kicked off a little further away from him. He was holding a book and squinting hard at it.

I lifted my sunglasses and watched him slouching over the book that was open in both hands. A light breeze pulled locks of hair from behind his ears, where he would always tuck them, and they closed in around his face. He moved a slender hand from the book to fix his hair. It looked like he wasn't even aware of his movement. It had to be something he did a million times a day.

But I couldn't stand here watching him for too long. My feet were eager to carry me closer to him. They moved of their own accord and I kicked sand as I headed his way.

London looked up only when my shadow entered the sphere of his vision. The smile that broke out over his face was short, but it was genuine. Then, he wrinkled his lips and nose in a mock pout. "Next time you buy me a book, make sure it's got at least one gay sex scene in it or don't waste your money."

I laughed out loud. "I don't know about you, but *Micro to Macro* sounds a little like an ad you get on porn sites."

"Grandpa Moe's dick enlargement trick?" London shook his head at me. "That's all great, but the subtitle says *Economics Explained*. And that's just a buzz kill."

I dropped my stuffed backpack into the sand and sat on London's jacket as he scooted over a little. "How about I bring some buzz back to life?"

London let his head hang back and closed his eyes, taking in the sunshine. His face was so radiant that it almost looked like he was showering the sun and not the other way around. "I'm already in the most beautiful place in the world," he said slowly, eyes still closed. His lips ticked up into a smile. "And with the most beautiful guy," he added in a whisper.

"I can do better," I said and nudged him with my elbow.

London laughed. He opened his eyes and looked at me. He knew not to kiss me in public even if he wanted to. I wished I could just get over it all and kiss him here, but the mental break was ever-present. I wanted to stow him away with me and have him where nobody could find us.

But I didn't want to wait.

I licked my lips and looked away. "I hope you don't have any plans," I said.

"What if I do?" he teased.

I knew he had none. We'd already talked about having this evening off. I'd just never specified *where*. And it wasn't going to be here. "Oh, do you?" I intentionally dropped my voice lower because it never failed to make him blush.

"I might," he said and suppressed the growing grin.

"And do those plans involve me?" I teased.

"They could." His gaze met mine for a split second before he looked up all innocently.

"How about we make sure they do?" I asked and let my cool and cocky mask slip. Underneath it, a grin was emerging. I pulled my phone out, unlocked it, and found the photo of the place I'd booked. Then, I handed him my phone. "How's that?"

London shrugged, fake unimpressed. "Since the plans are to learn these formulas by heart, I guess it's as good as any place."

I laughed at that and he joined me. "I'll make sure to motivate you."

He cocked an eyebrow. "Are you for real?"

"I'm not known for my devious pranks," I said. "I'm for real." I glanced at the backpack in the sand. "And I have all you're gonna need right here."

"Swimming shorts included?" he joked.

I snorted. "Nope. But all my notebooks are coming along."

London shook his head in disbelief again. "But seriously? You just want to...go?"

"Why not? We can be there in three hours." I took my phone from him. "I'm booking a car."

London laughed. "Three hours is a long drive."

Oh, I was aware of that. "I'll make you a deal, though."

London stuck two fingers inside his tie and loosened it a little. "Yeah?" His chest rose as he took a deep breath.

"Use those three hours to read my notes and we'll do a quiz when we get there," I said.

"So romantic," he replied, so sarcastic that it almost sounded genuine.

By now, the muscles in my face were hurting from all the smiling. "Each question you get right..."

He leaned in, eyes widening, pupils dilating.

"I'll take a piece of clothing off," I finished.

London swallowed hard and squirmed on his suit jacket. "And if I get it wrong?" he asked, voice strangled.

"If you plan on getting them wrong, you really should have that jacket on instead of under you," I said with a laugh.

London bit his lip shortly, then nodded. "I'm in. Where's the car?"

I glanced at my phone. "Oh... It just arrived."

Three hours really were a long drive, even in a business-class car as large and comfortable as the one I'd hired on the go. And while I observed the hills and valleys around us, London, a true and passionate economist and a future career businessperson, never lifted his gaze off my notebooks. Or, maybe he really wanted to see me naked. The thought sent a wave of heat rising to my face, but it also thrilled me to my marrow.

I had no problem handing him my phone. With London, I had no reason to keep secrets or fear being found out about anything. But when it came to notebooks in my backpack, I was careful to keep it out of his sight. Not that I had any big secrets in there, but I didn't want to frighten him or add my expectations onto him; the full bottle of lube and an unopened box of XXL condoms were sort of a clear hint at what I hoped would happen. But, I kept it from him, because it didn't really matter if it didn't happen. I just didn't want him thinking that sex was the only reason we were headed up there. But it would be a pretty big plus. So, I was ready and hopeful.

I'd done my practical experiment what felt like ages ago. And I did all my theoretical research afterward. And finally, I did what the online guides and tutorials talked about today. If there ever was a chance for a spontaneously planned evening of steam, it was tonight.

Three hours later, the expansive, hilly, walled-off area came into sight. The gates opened at the mention of my name with a quick look-up of my reservation and the voice from the intercom directed the driver to our final destination. The entire camp was all stylized nature, brimming with blooming bushes and thick evergreens to give each cabin plenty of privacy. It wasn't advertised as such, but it was very much a place for couples to hide and go at it until they have no stamina left. However, it was advertised as a romantic getaway.

We stopped at the reception desk in one small cabin and I picked up the key to ours. Twenty-two, it said.

The cabins were identical in their purposes, though I couldn't really see their designs. I supposed they varied, but they were hidden deep in the trees and bushes that all I ever saw were bits and pieces of roofs or wooden walls.

The car slowed down to a halt in front of a small, wooden sign with the number '22' painted on it. That was us. The driver pressed a button that immediately sent me a notification to my phone. I glanced at it and noticed London smirking. *Daddy's got you covered*. He'd said that once, weeks ago, and the memory squeezed my insides. Dad really did have me covered, but I wasn't sure if that would be the case once the truth was out. He might very well cut me off and I wasn't ready yet.

I chose to forget all about my dad. Instead, I snatched my backpack and got out of the car. London followed, one of the notebooks still in his hands. "Shoot. I didn't even bring my pajamas," he said.

I chuckled. "Then, better make sure you know all the answers."

"We're really doing this?" he asked with an amused laugh.

"Hell yeah," I said, my excitement sparking to life again.

The car slowly moved away from us and London followed me casually down the narrow, paved path between the trees and bushes toward the entrance door. Standing outside our cabin felt almost like we were standing in the loneliest, most isolated place in the world. There were no sounds beyond the birds singing and the leaves and pine needles rustling in the light breeze. Every scent I inhaled was fresh and clean, fragrant with early fall bloom.

And the cabin itself was a small structure, but perfectly suitable. It had a single window in the front, next to the door on the ground floor, and another, smaller, round window high above the door.

I pushed the key in, turned it, and entered the cabin. It was as cozy as I had hoped. The ground floor area consisted of a spacious living room and a kitchen with an island that doubled as a dining table. There was a door in the back and a short hallway leading out on the patio where there was supposed to be a hot tub. Up in the loft was the sleeping area. It wasn't exactly a room, though it had balustrades to protect us from falling into the living room.

There was a large TV mounted onto the wall across from the sofa to my right.

"This is nice," I said and walked over to the kitchen. Though it had a stove, it also had a neatly placed menu on the island so that we could order our food. Other than that, there was a microwave, a coffee maker, a small fridge, and plenty of glasses for various beverages.

"Holy crap," London said and shut the door behind him.

Across the room, beyond the sofa and the TV, there was a large window letting in plenty of sunlight. But on each side of the window, there were thick curtains that we could pull closed if we wanted extra privacy.

"Is that a good holy crap?" I joked.

"Uh, the best holy crap money can buy," London said with a smirk that begged to be kissed and licked and bitten.

I had to root myself to this spot to refrain from going to him. Dragging it out would feel so much better, I reminded myself.

I walked around the living room, dropped my backpack on the floor, then crashed onto the sofa to test its sturdiness. "Not bad at all," I said with a thick note of pride. I'd impressed London Reynolds; not many people could say that.

London circled the living room and loosened his tie some more, then popped the top button of his pristine white shirt. The dark red pants that were part of our uniforms matched his striped, red and white socks, and he wore plain white sneakers. His suit jacket, sandy from misuse, was folded in his right hand. He threw it over the high chair by the kitchen island, then spun around and leaned against the counter with a mischievous smile emerging on his face. "I'll bet you anything that you'll regret making me that deal," he said.

My heart thumped harder. I wasn't going to regret anything. "We shall see. You're still green in the way of economics, even if you're better than you were a month ago."

"I love it when you talk dirty to me," he said sarcastically.

I snorted. "You haven't heard half of it."

He made a *tss* sound between his teeth like what I'd said revealed some super secret kink to him. It made my chest shake with laughter.

I reached for my backpack and pulled out a folder of freshly printed sample quizzes. I'd compiled some that I could think of specifically for London. Then, I tucked the backpack away, and glanced at London. "So, you're ready?"

He pumped himself up by blowing some air out of his lungs and shaking his fists. "As ready as I'll ever be." He crossed the small room and dropped onto the floor, legs folded under his sweet ass and elbows on his knees.

I slid off the sofa to the floor, too, and placed the folder with all the papers on top of the small coffee table between us. The answers on my quizzes weren't marked for correct ones. After all, I knew this stuff like the back of my hand.

But before I began with the first question, something made me look up. Our gazes locked, eyes a little narrow. His pupils dilated and he looked like he wasn't breathing. I sure wasn't breathing, either. Who needed air when they could have London Reynolds? There was no room for anything else but him.

We gazed at one another with all the wanting and desperate need for more, all tucked neatly behind our eyeballs, but all growing rapidly. His long face, his jaw-length locks of hair, his slanted, brown eyes, and his slender, long neck with a visi-ble Adam's apple rising and falling as he swallowed made me wish I'd found harder questions just so I could undress him sooner.

I licked my lips. "Uh...management decision problems are comprised of three things. Which of the following *isn't* one of them?" I asked and cleared my throat. He was so fucking beautiful that I was sweating. What the hell was he doing crushing on me? He only had to look at someone to have them wrapped around his little finger, yet he decided to come here with me. "Profitability; alternatives; objectives; or constraints?"

London narrowed his eyes in thought. "Alterna-tives?"

"Is that a question or an answer?" I asked, mim-icking the usual, patronizing voice a professor might use. London got the joke and sneered, then laughed.

"It's an answer," he said pointedly.

"Hmm," I said and leaned over the coffee table, then closed my hand around his red and gold tie. "I think I'll have the tie." My fingers ran down its length as I gently pulled it toward me.

London scoffed. "You must be wrong."

"Nope. The correct answer is profitability. Con-trary to your skeptical, and a little stereotypical, belief that management only ever wants profits, profitability is *not* one of the decision problems." I lifted a corner of my lips in a victorious smirk.

My heart tittered when London rolled his eyes and pulled the collar of his tie far enough to take the whole thing off over his head. He held the knot in his tight fist and handed me the tie. The narrow, red and gold strip of fine silk cloth dangled in the air and I took it with pride. "I will just say that this is highly debatable, but here, have it."

I snickered and brought the tie to my nose just to rub the loss in. I didn't expect that catching the whiff of London's cologne on the tie would send my heart into overload. Sparks burst through my chest as I inhaled.

London half-suppressed a smile, lowered his head and shook it, then lifted a manicured black eyebrow at me. "Is that it or do you have more questions?"

I laughed softly. "I have plenty." Another glance at the paper made me think I already had the next one in the bag. Would it be the shoes? Would it be the socks? "Which of the following areas of economics is the single most important element of ME? Mathematical economics; macroeconomics; or microeconomics?" I smiled, feeling cocky a bit too soon.

"Microeconomics," London spelled out. "And I think that'll cost you your underwear." His grin was fucking vicious.

My eyes widened. "Underwear? I've got like five other things to take off first." I lifted his tie. "I'll make you a deal. How about you take your tie back instead?"

He shook his head. "Underwear or we're leaving," he said with a mock-pout.

"That's..." I lost the rest of my thoughts. My cock stirred at the thought and I was having serious trouble with the flow of air.

"Not against the rules," he pointed out. "Skedaddle to the bathroom, take them off, put your shorts

back on, and hand them over, soldier. I'm fond of
the idea that you'll be sitting here commando for
the rest of the game."

Skedaddle to the bathroom, I thought and chuckled
to myself. Nah. I had a better solution. "Fine," I said
in a playful growl. Swiftly, I got up and loosened
my shoulders like I was getting ready for a boss
fight in *Seeds of Soulless*.

If he wanted me to go away, undress, and come
back, he was sorely underestimating me. I hooked
my thumbs inside my shorts, then met his gaze.

London's eyes widened a little as I lifted a corner of my lips into a half-smile, bent down, and
dragged my shorts down to my ankles. I kicked my
shoes off and got out of my shorts. I turned away
from London just to tease him harder. Yeah, I had
no mercy or pity for him.

Slowly, I pulled my boxer-briefs over my ass as
my dick tingled with my erection coming on. My
boxer-briefs dropped and I stepped out of them.
My dick was semi-hard as I turned halfway back
to London and bent down again to put the shorts
back on.

My gorgeous Apollo wheezed as I dragged this
action out. Our gazes met and I bit my lip, sliding
the waistband over my growing erection. Then, as
I picked my boxer-briefs up, a soft, pained whimper escaped London's lips.

As I sat back down, I hooked my boxer-briefs
over my index finger and handed them to London.

Yet, what made me twist around to get the re-
mote for the AC unit in the room and bring the
temperature down, was London's cheeky grin and
dirty mind. He stared into my eyes as he imitated

my exact gesture from earlier. He took my under-wear off my finger and brought them to his face, tightened his grip on the fabric, and buried his nose into them. He never once took his eyes off of me as he took a deep breath.

When he was done, he made his eyebrows jump up and down once. "Lavender softener. You might really be gay."

"Fuck. Me." I wheezed.

London cackled and raised his finger after drop-ping my underwear on the far end of the coffee table. "Soon enough," he said cheekily. "But first, a question. You said you wanted me to fuck you back in the library. Do you mean, like...top you?"

I gulped on empty air and opened my mouth. "Shit. Sorry. I don't mean to offend you. And I don't mean to assume. I read that some guys have strong preferences and some don't. I never asked you if...like...maybe..."

London laughed softly. It was the most melodic, most soothing laugh I could imagine. "I'm versa-tile. Equal measures, really. The reason I'm asking is pure curiosity. Cos you made it sound like you *really* want to bottom." He added another laugh that relaxed me further.

I shrugged. It wasn't like I didn't want to fuck London. Just thinking about holding his narrow waist and thrusting into him, catching his whim-pers into my mouth, and running my hands over his flat chest was enough to make my dick throb. But it was the idea of London carefully push-ing into me, eyes locked, breaths low, that really stirred every shred of me. "I don't know if I have a preference, it's just..." Why the hell was it still so hot inside? "I kinda really like the idea of... You doing it."

London laughed. "I made you blush." He shook his head a little. I learned quickly that London shaking his head was a sign of affirmation, satisfaction, and even encouragement. "Next question, please."

It took me a moment to pull myself out of the daydream of coiling in that bed up in the loft with a naked and horny London, but I glanced at the papers in my folder and returned to the present. "Uh-huh. Right. Here goes." I cleared my throat. "Firms don't continue to grow without limit because of: managerial limitation; antitrust laws; or income tax?"

London nodded as he thought about it. "Antitrust laws," he said.

"That's an obvious answer," I said to his broadening smile. He inhaled as if to ask me to remove another bit of clothing, but I beat him to it. "Except that it's wrong. Managerial limitations."

"Fuck. I knew that," he said and cursed again under his breath. "What do you want?"

"Sneakers. See? I play fair." I smiled at him as he kicked his sneakers off, then pushed them with his foot over to my side. "Thank you very much. I will not, in fact, be sniffing them."

He laughed. "Good. I still want you to like me."

Like seemed like a weak word for what soared through my chest, but I swallowed the words and returned to the papers. "Ah. The modern theories hold that firms behave in a way to maximize which of the following? Profit; revenue; monopoly; or the value of the firm?"

"Revenue. By extent, that will increase profits and value and give them a shot at a monopoly." London crossed his arms at his chest and glanced down my torso, or what was visible above the coffee table, at least.

I shook my head. "Did you actually read anything in the last three hours?" I teased. "Spend a million dollars this year to increase the revenue from half a million to eight hundred thousand and everything will collapse. You're gonna go bankrupt."

"This game sucks," he said.

"The answer is, the value of the firm. It can be increased by acquiring modern equipment, increasing profits, and a million other ways. Revenue is secondary if you can double the value of your company in a year." I smiled to soften the lecturing, but London rolled his eyes.

"Socks?" he asked.

"Nah. Gimme that pretty shirt of yours," I said.

He blew out a long breath of air as he undid the buttons top-down and revealed more and more of his sexy torso. I fucking loved his sculpted torso. Every bit of it was so delicately defined. It showed that London stuck to a healthy routine at the gym and his swimming habits, which he preferred, made all the difference.

I took the shirt from him and tossed it onto the sofa where London's tie lay. "Next. Which of the firm's functional areas has the highest responsibility for revenue? Finance; marketing; personnel."

London narrowed his eyes. "You're just asking that so I can score a point and you don't have to deal with a sore loser."

I laughed out loud and turned the folder to him. "Nope. The question's right here."

"Marketing," he said.

"Well done." I hooked a finger inside my T-shirt and London nodded. Swiftly, I pulled it over my head and tossed it across the table.

London caught my T-shirt and balled it in his hands, then held it all the while scanning my chest. My muscles were much larger than his, shoulders broader and arms thicker. There was a little hair around my nipples and some rare hair down the middle of my chest, and then some more under my belly button, leading toward my pants. Though I was mostly smooth, I was still in contrast with London, who looked like he'd had laser removal done. I doubted that was the case, but he was all tanned skin and no hair.

I wondered if he knew it, but he bit his bottom lip and seemed to have forgotten all else.

"Which of the following terms is associated with negotiating and enforcing a contract? Functional cost; opportunity cost; or transactional cost?" I gazed at him, but he still had his eyes on my torso and teeth firmly around his lip.

He sighed. "Imma go ahead and say, opportunity cost."

"And now, go ahead and hand me those pants because it's called transactional cost." I grinned as London reluctantly pushed himself up and undid the button, then unzipped the dark red pants.

I held my breath as he teasingly dragged out the entire process. He turned so that I would watch his profile and pulled his pants over his ass, revealing, once again, that he wore tight briefs. These were bright blue with black line art boats. Maybe they weren't as sinful as the last pair, but they sure fit him nicely. In the front, London's crotch was large and growing. I guessed his cock was still fairly soft, but it filled the briefs to their maximum capacity. His balls were big enough to keep the edge of his briefs ever so slightly away from his groin. There, too, he was as smooth as if hair had never grown out. His androgynous beauty made my heart perform a drum solo in my ears.

London bent down and pulled his pants to his ankles, then finally handed me my prize. Now, I was the one staring helplessly. My cock was as hard as it could get, pitching a tent out of my briefs, and throbbing as I watched London slowly descend back to the floor.

"Last question," I said in a strangled voice. My fingers trembled as I placed them on top of the folder and lifted my gaze to meet his brown eyes. A shade of pink dusted his cheeks in the sexiest of ways and I inhaled. "Do you, maybe, wanna take this to another level?" The words were out of me quickly, like ripping off an adhesive bandage.

London glanced shortly at the loft. "Literally or metaphorically?" he teased.

"Both."

He narrowed his eyes at me. "If I get this answer right, say goodbye to those shorts, mister."

"I sure hope I will." I managed a little laugh with that, but frankly, all I felt was the need to press my body against his and let our passion burn everything that stood in its way.

London slowly got up again and extended his arm toward me. His open hand waited for a moment, then I grabbed it and let him help me up to my feet.

He walked in front of me, answering me without any words. And just before we were too far, I snatched my backpack with my other hand and carried it with us.

"Those better not be notebooks you're bringing," he said in a mock-annoyed voice.

But I couldn't think about a clever reply. I could hardly even stand. My gaze followed his broad upper back, the line of his spine, the narrowness of his waist, and the roundness of the curve of his ass.

The dark blue edges of his otherwise light and vibrant briefs had moved up his cheeks and were dangerously close to the middle. They really were very small and that alone made my thirst for his body ten times harder.

As London climbed the stairs toward the loft, I watched his hips swing, ass move, and muscles in his legs tense.

And then, in no time, we were in the loft by the bed, and London was turning around to face me. My gaze was still down there and I found that his crotch had gotten bigger. His cock was growing toward his left hip, stretching the already tight fabric, and begging for my lips.

"Is this the correct answer?" he asked when I looked into his eyes.

I reached between us and undid the button on my shorts, carefully unzipped them, and let them drop around my ankles. My cock stood upright and not a trace of shame remained in me. Around him, I never wanted to wear anything at all. "Flying colors," I purred as I stepped out of my shorts.

London carefully put his hand on the side of my ribcage and gazed into my eyes. "You can kiss me now."

I didn't let a moment pass. We were here on borrowed time and every second spent not kissing this angel was a second I would never get back. We were in a place of absolute freedom of thoughts and opinions, judgments and punishments. He was, in the truest sense of it, the center of my world here.

I tossed my backpack onto the bed. My hands landed on his hips and tugged him close, pressing his body against mine. He parted his lips for the impact and I kissed him hungrily.

His fingers, on the side of my torso, dug into my skin; more so the harder I kissed him.

I wrapped my arm around him and pulled him closer still, trapping him against my body.

He let out a little moan at the same time as he moved his hips and rubbed his trapped, hard cock against my leg. The move meant that his lower abdomen was sliding along the length of my dick and the sensation sent shivers up my spine.

Without thinking, I moved my head away from him, buried my face in his neck, and showered him with kisses. Hastily, I kissed and bit and licked him everywhere down his chest and stomach until I found myself on my knees.

I wrapped my left hand around my cock and felt the slickness of precum covering it. My grip was loose and the pulls were slow and relaxed. Any

harder and I would blow way before getting all that
my heart desired.

London's head dropped back and he ran his
fingers through my hair as I kissed his abdomen
and lowered myself further. My lips found the
base of his cock, kissing the cotton briefs and the
throbbing thickness underneath them. Disorient-
ed and needy for anything and everything I could
get, I dragged my lips over his packed balls, then
along the length of his dick until I reached the tip
that was pushing the briefs off his hip. There, I
let myself playfully bite him, using the fabric as a
softener against my teeth, and London hissed and
moaned, somehow both at once.

His grip on my short hair tightened and he
tugged me closer, pushing my face into his crotch.

My right hand closed around his ankle, then
slowly dragged up his leg until I found his ass.
There, I squeezed him firmly, making his cock
twitch with excitement. Smoothly, I slipped my
fingers under his briefs, feeling the softness of
his skin. Deeper my fingers went until they found
their way between his cheeks and a thought
flashed through my mind; soon enough, London's
fingers would do the same to me.

I let go of my cock. The thought was too hot to
allow me to keep stroking myself. The excitement
ran too high. If I weren't very careful, this would
end before it really got going.

But the willpower required to not touch myself
while kissing the tip of his cock was burning me
out. It was like lifting a car with nothing but bare
hands.

I used my now free hand to hook the edge of his briefs under my fingers and lift it over his cock. Though I'd had it in my mouth once already, and in my hand the day after that, it still made my heart flicker to see it in front of my face. The intimidating nine inches rose in front of me, swinging left and right for a moment before standing as upright as the weight allowed.

A shivering breath later, the need for his body overwhelmed any and every fear and doubt and I pulled his underwear down his legs with one rough stroke. I wrapped my fingers around the base of his dick and closed my lips around a mouthful. Sucking him in, taking in the salty taste, inhaling the faint, sweet musk of his body, silenced the last of my reservations. He was finally mine.

London's murmurs and moans encouraged me to try and take more of him. I relaxed my throat and pushed my head down on his cock, extended my lips further, and let saliva trickle down his length.

He tightened his grip on my hair again, dragging me back, then closer still. He used my mouth for his pleasure and fuck if it didn't please me just as much.

I cupped his balls, obsessed with their size and weight and smoothness, in my other hand. My index and middle fingers found his taint and rubbed it, happy to feel the twitch in his cock.

Daring to test how far this game could go, I let those fingers slide further along his taint until I found the warmth between his cheeks. He'd said he was versatile and he didn't lie. Merely touching his hole made his cock stiffen more in my mouth.

"Ah. Fuck," he whimpered and pushed my head away. "Keep doing that and you'll have to settle for a finger," he said with a soft chuckle and gazed deep into my eyes.

My mouth was hanging open and I was looking up at him, his cock a fraction of an inch away from my lips. My chest heaved as I had barely allowed myself to breathe while sucking him.

London lowered himself to his knees in the next instant and closed his hands around my face. His lips neared mine, then we connected. I barely held my orgasm back when I realized he must have tasted himself on my lips. He kissed and sucked and moaned into my mouth as his hand searched for my cock. There, he stroked me gently, building up the pressure and anticipation.

"How sure are you about bottoming?" he asked, an inch away from my lips.

"Never been so sure about anything in my life," I murmured.

His smirk was devious. "You already did some-thing there, didn't you?"

I chuckled as if to hide the creeping blush. "Maybe."

"A finger?" he asked and jerked my cock.

My balls tightened. "Yeah. Sure. A finger...at first."

"Gabriel," he said as if he was about to ask me the most serious question in the world. "Do you, perhaps, have a dildo?"

I snorted. "Does it matter what I used?" But my cock twitched in his hand at the memory of that afternoon.

"Humor me," he said, his grin growing.

I pursed my lips for a few heartbeats. "A cucumber."

His eyebrows shot up. "I was *not* expecting that, you pervy angel."

A laugh escaped the depths of my chest. It was a deep rumble that erupted when I threw my head back. But it was cut short; London stroked me again and my laughter turned to a whimper begging for some mercy. "Ah...um...you're still bigger."

Sparks burst out of his deep brown eyes. "It could hurt."

"I don't mind," I whispered.

"It could hurt a lot," he said, voice dropping lower.

I winced. The first time I tried to toy with the cucumber it hurt enough that I felt it in my eyes. "I still want to try," I said.

His nod was quick and jerky, his hand squeezing my pulsing cock. "Don't worry. I know how to make it painless."

I only lifted my eyebrows before he spoke again.

"Lie on your back, beautiful," he whispered seductively, then pressed his lips hard against mine. As he moved back, I followed, keeping my lips on his. And I followed him as we stood up.

As he had asked, I lay on my back on the large bed. The mattress was soft and my head sank into a heap of pillows.

London knelt between my spread legs and put one finger inside his mouth, the sight squeezing the last of the oxygen out of my lungs.

I lifted an invisible camera and did a little click just like he had the first time we fooled around.

He gave a low chuckle and reached for one of the pillows I wasn't using. "Lift that sexy ass," he said.

I did and he tucked the pillow under the small of my back.

"That feel good?" he asked.

"Uh-huh." I watched him as he returned his index finger inside his mouth and sucked it a little. "I...have lube," I said, brain swimming in a cocktail of lust and adrenaline.

"Tsk," he said as he pulled his finger out of his mouth. "We'll use it later."

His right hand wrapped around my dick and his left lowered under my balls. He cocked an eyebrow as if to ask if I was ready.

I gripped the bedsheets in my fists and curled my toes, then nodded.

London merely touched my hole with his index finger and all of me tensed.

A corner of his sexy lips lifted. "Easy," he whispered. "Just relax."

I nodded.

"And tell me to stop or slow down," he said, his voice returning to normal for that one moment.

"I will," I said. "I'm ready."

His finger circled my hole, rubbing and massaging until slowly but surely my muscles loosened and he felt it. His finger, slick with his saliva, slipped into me painlessly. Not a sliver of discomfort made itself known. No; it was like taking my first flight or like jumping off a cliff into the safety of the ocean.

His finger entered me slowly, but it went deep. The further he pushed, the easier it seemed to go. Though my lips had formed a wide O and my brow was furrowed, I breathed quickly and kept the eye contact going.

A small smile touched London's handsome face. "That's a good boy," he said.

Fuck. That sounded hot. I jerked my head as if to nod, but London began pulling his finger out as slowly as he had pushed it in. My dick pulsed and hole tightened momentarily, but London was already in control of me. His hand changed the movement and he entered me again. Again and again and again, he got me used to the motion and the lack of control over the movement. It had been one thing to do it myself, and a totally different feeling of having two useless hands by my hips while he penetrated me with his finger.

"Now, we could use that lube," he said as he pulled his finger out. It was a quick move of his hand and my hole closed tightly, but I longed for his finger immediately.

I rummaged in haste through my backpack with my right hand and pulled out the unopened pack of condoms and a new bottle of lube.

"You weren't kidding," London said.

"Never do," I said, catching my breath at last.

He picked up the bottle, slicked his index and middle fingers, then met my gaze. "Level up," he joked.

I nodded and pushed my head deeper into the pillows.

The way his biceps tensed as he pressed his fingers against my hole without pushing them in caught my eye. His chest flexed, too, and his abs seemed sharper, more defined. He really was holding back, careful not to hurt me.

Empowered by his behavior, I lifted my right hand and closed it around his wrist. Our eyes locked on one another and I winced as I jerked his hand into myself. This way, I felt freer to push the limits without any fear. Even if only a little, I was in control, thus I was responsible.

London's two fingers slid in quickly. And though it still didn't hurt, I definitely felt more than before. I felt the stretching of the muscle and the fullness that his fingers brought into my body.

But as soon as London pulled his hand back, then pushed it deeper in, those sensations lowered in intensity. I was slick and relaxed as he fingered me for a solid couple of minutes. Each thrust sent a wave of lust-coated chills through my body.

"Fuck," I murmured. "This feels good."

"Want more?" he asked, a little more sure about himself.

"Hell yeah," I whispered.

He didn't need more lube, so he didn't pull his fingers out. Instead, he stopped moving his hand and I let go of his wrist. He pressed his third finger against my hole and waited, eyes on me and ablaze. His jaw clenched as he pushed his third finger into me and I sucked air through my teeth.

Once he was in, I breathed a sigh of relief, and reveled in the stretching and finger-fucking he unleashed upon me. The pace intensified; the pressure grew. He shoved his three fingers into me again and again.

Each thrust was accompanied by a grunt from his lips and a moan from mine.

"Fuck, London, please." I didn't know what I was begging for. I just knew that it sounded correct. "I need your dick, London. Right. Fucking. Now."

He pushed his fingers in right to his knuckles, hitting my pleasure spot and making me gasp for air. "My dick's still bigger than this."

"I know," I gasped. "Just fuck me already."

"If you say so," he said with an ambiguous smile and carefully pulled his fingers out.

While I breathed and fought the urge to toy with my cock until an early climax, London slipped a condom on and poured plenty of lube into his hand, then stroked himself for a little while.

He nodded at me and I managed a jerky nod back.

Lifting my legs up and holding them under the knees, I focused all of my attention on his sparkling eyes.

London towered over me. His closed fist sank into the pillows next to my head. His other hand was on his cock, stroking it evenly. He navigated his cock between my cheeks while keeping his gaze on my eyes. The tip touched my hole and my entire body shivered with excitement. This was it. This was what I'd wanted him to do all along. My first proper time with my sexy Apollo.

He waited without pushing until he sensed me relaxing. Then, carefully, he pushed the tip in, mouth falling open in unison with mine.

My hands clasped behind his neck, calves of my legs resting on his shoulders, as he sank his dick slowly deep inside of me.

"Fuck, you're tight," he growled, still pushing.

The moment when he properly entered me was when the last shred of pain dissolved and my hole squeezed around his cock.

"Is that..." I panted. "Is that bad?" It wasn't supposed to be. But I knew the rules for straight sex a tad better than these.

His smile meant I had said something silly. "Oh, no. It's fucking perfect. That's what it is." He bit his lip and thrust his hips forward, his thick cock hitting my prostate and making mine pulse and drip with precum.

I kept my hands on his neck, sliding my thumbs around and holding him gently. The baring of the teeth said he liked what I was doing, so I gave a little squeeze. Though soft, the squeeze of his neck made his hips jerk back and forth harder. He stabbed at me faster, his balls swinging back and forth, touching my ass each time his cock impaled me deeper.

His abs kept flexing as he put them to work. His hands pressed against my broad chest and limited me in how deeply I could inhale.

Push after push after push, London's cock reached inside and stretched me more than any fucking cucumber could. Beads of sweat collected over his forehead and the first trickle ran down the side of his face. A drop fell from him onto me and I felt its tiny splash.

Every cell in me inflated. Every bit of me bloomed and expanded. I was a thousand feet tall and growing.

My hands tightened around his neck and his found mine. He never choked me; not even for an instant. But the grip tightened enough that I truly felt it.

My hands dropped from his neck and felt his chest with hunger that was only awake in moments of passion. I wished I could lick the sweat off his chest. I wished I could somehow bend and reach the precum slick tip of my cock with my own tongue.

Yet all I could do was grunt and moan and plead for more. "Please." Again, again. "Please, London."

London pushed his knees into the mattress harder, as if getting ready for something. Then, he slowly pulled his dick almost all the way out, met my gaze, held it for a heartbeat, then shoved it deeper into me.

I felt every thick inch of him. I felt every last pulse of his cock and I reacted by clawing for his chest.

His casual lip-biting fanned the fire in my body and I spun us around. London fell onto his back, his dick sliding out of me as he did. But I was on top of him moments later.

As he dropped, he let his arms fall above his head. He didn't move them. He only smirked, the horny devil. His chest heaved as I sat on him and took his cock in my hand.

I held him steadily upright and inched back on my knees until the tip was pressed against my hole. This movement required all my inner strength as much as the work of my muscles. I lifted myself inches above it, sat in a way that his dick was perfectly straight and aimed it at my hole, then I impaled myself on his nine fucking inches like it was the line between life and death.

I growled as I slid down his length and felt him push into me.

He'd waited with his arms above his head all along. But now, he reached down and spread my cheeks, held me so that I wouldn't sit any lower, and allowed his hips some room to move vertically.

And then, he blew my mind.

His muscles tensed as he thrust his hips up and down, fucking me blind. His abdomen met my balls each time his ass jumped off the bed to strike me harder.

Sweat trickled down my chest and back. Precum dripped lazily from my cock, thick and connected to where it pooled under London's small belly button.

He fucked me harder and faster, pushing against my prostate to the point where I was left simply gasping for air, unable to cry out or beg for more.

"You're going to come," he said, voice deeper than usual.

"Yes," I hissed as I closed my hand around my aching length.

He increased his pace and I wondered, distantly, where he was drawing this stamina from. He looked like he could go all night.

London snatched my free hand away from his chest and sucked in my index finger all the while I stroked myself, ready for the sweet release.

When my finger was wet, he pulled it out of his mouth. "Put it in my ass."

My eyes widened in a brief moment of surprise, but a smile followed.

London never stopped pounding me, though he slowed down in the moment when my finger brushed against his crack. There, I found the warm, pulsing hole and mercilessly pushed my finger into him.

London's lips parted and head sank deeper into the mattress. His chest seemed to rise, back arching up. He allowed me to push my finger all the way in before he began speeding up his upward thrusts.

My balls rose and tightened as I stroked my dick and jerked my finger in and out of my lover.

An instant followed in which nothing at all happened. Everything stopped. Everything was quiet. I saw myself laying in grass in an open field under the sun. I saw myself rolling to my side and finding a naked London, smiling bright. I saw myself leaning in and pressing my lips against his.

And sparks burst.

And fireworks lit the night sky.

And everything moved once again.

The incredible pressure that had gathered on my chest and in every cell of my body exploded in the culmination of our passion.

My orgasm thundered through me. It tensed and relaxed each of my muscles individually. But, at the exact same time, London's hole tightened rapidly around my finger and his dick throbbed inside of me, filling the condom.

Cum shot out of my swollen dick in heaps and with the sort of strength I hadn't been aware of. Drops splashed London's chin and he grunted an 'oh fuck,' before sticking his tongue out and reaching for it, then grinning at me.

My brain swam in lust and my cock pumped more of my hot wetness at the sight of his kinky delight.

London quickly dragged his finger along his cum stained chest and pushed it into his mouth.

Our movements slowed down with ease and he pulled his dick out, making me wince for a moment with an oddly new sensation. It wasn't bad, but it wasn't the best feeling either, now that I had finished.

"Want a taste?" he asked as I climbed off of him and lay by his side.

He still toyed with scattered pools of my cum on his torso.

I saw the eager smile behind the indifferent mask he wore and did him one better. Instead of licking it off his finger, I leaned in and pressed my tongue against the middle of his chest, then cleaned a small pool of my whiteness off his skin.

Swallowing it slowly, I found I actually enjoyed it. But before I could do anything else, London clasped my face and pulled me in for a hot kiss, tongues rubbing against one another, searching for the remains of my orgasm in each other's mouth.

He breathed heavily after the kiss and gazed into my eyes. "Still can't find your limits," he said in a tone that fell somewhere between a tease and admiration.

"You'll just have to look harder," I said.

He smiled and nodded, then pulled me down for a long period of cuddling, caressing, and simply holding each other.

You'll just have to look harder. Or maybe, when I'm with you, I don't have a limit to be found.

CHAPTER TEN
Double Date Fakers

OUR DREAM QUICKLY CAME to an end. It only lasted a night and a morning. Oh, but it was a busy night and an even busier morning. We had barely managed to order food and dip our naked asses in the hot tub on the back patio, in between this whole business of looking for Gabriel's limits.

The only thing I found was an endless source of lust. It matched mine to a tee.

The car picked us up around noon when we were supposed to check out and dropped us off near the beach where it had found us the day before.

I gazed at the ocean and the longing for its steady, infinite waves awoke in me.

"Come on. I need a swim," I said and gestured for the beach.

"You were in a hot tub just this morning," he protested, abashed.

"Darling. Honey. Sweetie. You're the one who decided to date a fish." I snickered and laughed out loud to hide the fact that I was blushing after slipping and saying we were dating.

Gabriel's full, red lips stretched into a goofy smile.

"What?" I asked, eyebrows flat and eyes ready to roll.

He shrugged. "You said we're dating. I like that."

"Shut up," I grunted. This had a perfect place in all the novels I had under my bed, but it was too weird to hear in real life.

"You don't have anything to swim in," he pointed out.

"Hmpf. I know a place where I don't need any. Besides, I can swim in my briefs. They're not made of paper." I tugged his short sleeve briefly, then let go. We still hadn't moved toward anything public, which was totally fine with me. We didn't need to rush it.

Even if he liked the idea of us dating.

"Ah, I guess it's my fault for dating a fish," he echoed and cracked a smile.

Jitters surged up from my stomach as he started to follow me.

We descended the short stairs from the promenade to the sandy beach and walked up, but I spotted my sister in the distance. She was lounging under a large umbrella with a cocktail in her hand and big, black sunglasses hiding her eyes.

"That's Elle," I said. A little twist crept into my guts and I bit my lip. "Should we say hi?" I'd talked to Elle over the phone, but I hadn't seen her since the day she scolded me. And I was pretty sure Gabriel would have told me had he seen her.

"Sure," he said casually.

I seemed to be the only one who feared this turning awkward. But as we headed towards Elle, I realized she was talking.

The terrace of the beach bar extended far and wide and I hadn't been able to tell the distances from afar. But now, as we were paces away, I realized that Elle was lounging on one side of the small table, and there was a guy on the other side.

"Who's that?" I whispered to Gabriel just as Elle noticed us and grinned. She lifted her sunglasses to the top of her head and waved.

"My boys," she said excitedly from the lounger. She leaned in to the guy who had most of his torso covered in ridiculously awesome ink, all the way along his neck and to his jawline, and had a pierced nose, said something, then got up to meet me and Gabriel.

She threw her arms around both of us at once and kissed our cheeks in turn. "Look how handsome you are together," she whispered.

I frowned. "What the hell happened to Elle, you terrible copy?"

She laughed out loud. "What do you mean?"

Gabriel chuckled. "She's happy, London."

"I don't like it," I said.

Elle let go of us and returned to the lounger. There were a few empty ones scattered around, so Gabriel and I dragged one each to their table.

"This is Zach," Elle said.

Zach, who, at first, seemed like a tough punk, hardly even noticed Gabriel and me. Instead, he was mooning over Elle like a cute puppy who just got a new human. "Hey guys," Zach said, glancing at us in turn.

We introduced ourselves and I started putting the pieces of the puzzle together.

Elle was happy.

Elle was with Zach.

Elle's ex was dating me.

My date's ex was my twin sister, who was dating Zach.

I'm sorry, but this is too much to compute. I shook my head at myself and returned to the present, where Gabriel was saying how we'd just picked up and went away yesterday.

"That's adorable," Elle said. I hadn't seen her like this in... Ever? Man, these two never should have dated. They were giggling like schoolgirls now that they were only friends and I hadn't seen either of them this happy since before they'd gotten together.

It was a relief, to be fair.

"There is one problem," Elle said and looked at Gabriel. "Mom and Dad still expect us to show up at their gala."

Gabriel smacked his brow. "Crap. I totally forgot about the gala."

I rolled my eyes. "That crap, again?" I shook my head. "I think I said I'd go, too. And they got half my friends and their families to join."

Elle's face twisted in guilt as she looked between the three guys around her. "I do have an idea and Zach's on board."

Why the hell is Zach on board? I was weary of whatever plan she had come up with. The last plan she'd concocted involved tutoring lessons with her boyfriend and look how that ended. Not that it was a bad outcome — it was fucking awesome — but it didn't really go according to plan.

Zach, who was on board apparently, nodded at Elle. He sent me an innocent look that probably meant the plan involved me in some way.

"We'll be there if we have to," Gabriel assured her. "It's just..." He looked at me and squirmed. He wasn't ready to come out to his dad.

"Well, that's just it," Elle said. "I never told anyone that we broke up."

I narrowed my eyes until I could barely see any of them. This wasn't going well at all. "Elle," I said carefully. "What's the plan?"

She bit her lip and let me simmer in anticipation for a heartbeat longer. "If Gabriel and I go as a couple, like both families think we are, we'll all buy ourselves the rest of the year before we have to break the news to them."

I nodded. "Okay." I sighed with relief. "That's not too bad. I'm not even sure if I want to go. You two can deal with it on your own and..."

"*But*," Elle emphasized and a boulder dropped onto my stomach. "You could take Zach as your date," she told me and my jaw dropped into the sand. "That way we each get to be with our guys after the party."

"Elle, you're mad," I whispered. Of course, Mom and Dad wouldn't approve of Zach. At least not at first and at a gala of this size. And especially not after only finding out about the breakup.

And totally, definitely not if everybody found out about Gabriel and me. "Don't you remember what happened when you put me in the same room with your boyfriend the last time?"

Elle laughed out loud and so did Gabriel.

"Are you saying that you would exchange me so quickly?" Gabriel teased. He genuinely found it hilarious for some fucking reason.

"Shut up," I husked. He knew I wouldn't.

"Just hear me out," Elle said. "Nobody will bat an eye if you bring a stranger to a gala. It's not gonna be your first time." She smirked. "And we both get our respective man in an all-star hotel. What could go wrong?"

I growled. A whole lot could go wrong. But she was right. I wanted to be with Gabriel every waking and sleeping minute of my life. I didn't want to lose an entire extended weekend because of a fundraiser. And she was also right about nobody looking twice at Zach if he was with me. After all, I was a certified fuckboy.

I shook my head in defeat. "Fine. You're right."

Elle squealed, Gabriel seemed happy, and Zach looked totally oblivious to everything except Elle. It appeared as if I was the only one who had a bad feeling about this.

Maybe, deep down, I worried about Elle and Gabriel pretending to be a couple. I didn't need to. She was the only one who had any actual reason to worry about handing me her boyfriend on a silver platter, even if I had no interest in anyone but Gabriel. Still, having to see them exchange love-filled glances and be the perfect couple they'd always been at such gatherings sat heavy with me.

So, after we had a round of drinks together, and I lost my appetite for swimming, Gabriel and I headed back to campus. Only then did I start the discussion again, simply to check in with him. "Are you really comfortable with this?"

"Yeah," Gabriel said, then scratched the back of his head. "I mean, I think you guessed I'm not planning on telling my dad about you the first chance I get."

The way he said it stung even if it didn't need to.

He noticed. "I'm sorry," he said.

"You're alright," I replied quickly. "And I don't mind sneaking around. I really don't."

He sighed. "It's just that I'm pretty sure I'll soon get disinherited once he knows."

"Fuck, man," I said for the lack of any better words. These summed it up nicely.

"Yeah, that's about right," he agreed. "You know he wasn't the warmest person when I was growing up. That's why I all but grew up at your place." He smiled at me as if pulling fond memories from the back of his mind. "But I'd be lying if I said I could afford to lose my cards and shiny stuff."

"I get that. I really do. But it's not like you and Elle can't go on your own and pretend far away from where I am. And far away from that guy Zach." I scoffed. The puppy-looking emo was all over my sister and it was too sweet to look at. "You're not worried about me faking it with an-other dude?"

Gabriel laughed. "London, I trust you. Com-pletely."

I raised my eyebrows, caught off guard.

He stopped walking and looked into my eyes. "How is this news to you?" he asked. "I mean, the things we did just last night." He laughed again. "Obviously, I trust you with my life."

"With your balls, maybe," I said, unable to resist.

His cheeks turned a little pink. The thing I'd done late last night had gotten him really excited and it had been as simple as closing my finger around his sack above his balls and applying pressure in small increments. He'd gone wild after a few minutes and came all over himself not long after I'd put my second finger inside of him.

"That, too," Gabriel said. "But I also trust you with a secret that could ruin me financially and cost me my education, not to mention my gaming setup."

I chuckled at the way he prioritized it. "And me?" I teased.

"No," he said. "That won't happen. Unless you find yourself in dire need of a sugar daddy. In which case, old, disinherited Gabriel won't be able to compete."

We both laughed and began moving again.

If he was sure, then I was sure.

I saw him to his dormitory and he surprised me by taking my hand near the stairs when nobody was around. He pinned me against one of the Roman Doric columns and pressed his lips hard against mine. It lasted a short time, but it was sweet as hell.

"I'll see you tonight," I said.

"Text you," he said.

I knew he would.

When I got to the common room in our dormitory that doubled as our frat house, Hudson clapped his hands from the armchair. "And here I was, about to start phoning the hospitals."

"I was out," I said with no further explanation. "Where is everybody?"

"You know what?" Hudson grinned. "Since you're like that, I'll just let you worry about everyone missing."

I rolled my eyes and reached for a can in the fridge, then dropped onto the sofa and wiggled my hips as I sank in. The warm feeling around my hole reminded me of Gabriel's three fingers working me this morning. We hadn't gotten to the bit where he would top me, but he said he probably would at some point. Apparently, taking me in was all the rave for him.

"Son of a bitch, you're dating someone," Hudson said in disbelief.

I caught myself smiling at nothing, then quickly pulled an emotionless mask on. "What? I'm not."

"Yes, you are," Hudson said. "Another fuckboy down."

I snorted. "I'm most certainly not dating anyone. And if you're looking for a romance story, you'd be better off finding a boyfriend of your own."

He found that hilarious. "Never gonna happen. I'm in a serious relationship with my one-night-stands."

"And I'm happily married to my right hand, though I sometimes cheat on it with my left," I said and shrugged. "Dating someone? Not me, a married man."

"Bullshit," Hudson said and sipped from his can.

I cracked mine open and took a long sip of the bitter-sweet coldness, thinking about Gabriel.

"You've been gone all night without a trace and as soon as you stop barking, you're smiling like a fool. Not only are you dating, but you're dating hard." He grinned harder. "Spill the beans, Reynolds."

"Mind your business, Blackwood."

He chuckled.

"Fine," I growled. "But you'll swear to me never to speak of this to anyone until the day we're both gray."

Hudson Blackwood crossed his heart. "On my honor."

I scoffed. "It's Gabriel."

Hudson was mid-sip when I said this and a mouthful of beer sprayed his torso and the coffee table in front of him. Then, he began to cough the drops that had gone down the wrong pipe. "What?" he wheezed.

"You heard me," I said.

"Elle's Gabriel? Your twin sister's boyfriend?" His jaw dropped to the floor.

"They're not dating," I explained. "And before you say anything, I'm not taking any mistaken twin jokes today."

He narrowed his eyes. "That monstercock didn't give you away?" he mumbled.

Yet again, I rolled my eyes. "He's working through some stuff about himself. He's gay, dude. And it's complicated."

Hudson dropped the act and shook his head sympathetically. "I don't think it's that complicated, my friend. You're in love."

My heart grew twice its size as I thought of loving Gabriel.

Holy shit, I really am.

CHAPTER ELEVEN

Calm Before The Storm

———— elle ————

I SWALLOWED THE KNOT in my throat and searched
for Elle's hand after we got out of the car and stood
in front of *Orbit*, a five-star resort north of Santa
Maria.

My hand grew slick with cold sweat when I spotted London with an arm over a lost and stiff Zach.
They were at the very entrance with Mr. Ron and
Mrs. Judy Reynolds. Zach was nodding furiously
at something the smiling, middle-aged couple was
saying and London turned his head as if he sensed
my presence. Or Elle's, more likely.

I squeezed Elle's hand and the first creeps of
doubt crawled into my heart. What did it feel like

for London to see this? Did he worry? Words of trust only went so far. All I could do was hope that he wouldn't doubt me.

Tonight, I would prove myself to him. Zach and I would swap rooms once the coast was clear and I would prove to London just how much I cared for him. Because I did; far more than I was able to put into words.

"Are you alright?" Elle asked.

The tension in my shoulders spread to my neck. "Perfect." I inhaled and held a breath of air as if to incite some courage.

Elle gave a gentle tug and I moved with her. We approached Zach and London, as well as Mr. Ron and Mrs. Judy Reynolds. London glanced at us.

"'Sup," he said with an uninterested nod.

Shit. It sucks to see his lack of interest, I thought. *It sucks to feel his indifference, even if it's fake.*

"Hey dude," I said. *Remember when we slept together seven fucking times in the cabin, just a week ago?* Those words, however, I did not say. Yet they were loaded in my mouth and caused a bead of sweat to appear on my brow.

"Elle. Gabriel," Ron Reynolds clapped his hands in delight. "Judy, the kids are all here."

I shook hands with him, making sure my grip was firm, as if a weak grip could blow my cover.

"I'm glad you came," he said.

I like spending time naked with your son, I thought and bit my tongue. Why the hell was this so hard? "We wouldn't miss it for the world."

I glanced at London, who had already turned away from us and whose mask was firmly in place. But his *boyfriend* for the day was gaping at Elle with those big, dark puppy eyes and I could have sworn he drooled.

She deserves it, I thought to myself. *Someone who'll worship her the way I never could.*

During the ride up here, I'd asked her quietly so the chauffeur wouldn't hear, if she was happy with Zach.

She'd shrugged openly, but smiled secretly. It was the Reynolds language for 'I'm over the Moon.'

"Such a beautiful couple, you two are," Judy Reynolds said as she hugged us in turn.

I really enjoy being on my knees for London, I didn't say. "Aw, thanks," I did say.

The late afternoon sunlight bathed the white facade of the hotel in old gold and the windows reflected the light.

"Should we just go inside? The heat is melting my makeup," Elle said and fanned herself. She was only wearing a touch of mascara and a tiny trace of lipstick.

"Yes, darling," I blurted.

London grunted and grabbed Zach's hand, then tugged him around so that he would face him instead of staring at Elle.

Elle walked first and I followed. The hotel lobby was a vast, minimally decorated area that had simple sofas, armchairs, and coffee tables scattered around. We passed through and I hardly noticed the vibrant red paint or the milling people.

"That went well," I murmured to Elle.

"Yeah, no, you totally nailed it," she said sarcastically, but chuckled to soften the blow.

"Was I...obvious?" I stammered.

"You were fine except that you're trembling. What's up?" she asked as she pressed the button to call us an elevator.

"Nothing," I said, fidgeting, then sighed. "It's just harder than I expected. I can't get him out of my head."

"Aw, beau," she said softly. "It's really cute."

I snorted.

"What? It is cute," she insisted. "You're madly in love with my little brother."

"Shut up," I whispered, breathless.

We got into the elevator, then found our room.

"London's is just across the hallway," Elle said cheekily.

My heart tittered. "Good," I said without letting my excitement show too much.

The evening's star musician, Ralph Nye, serenaded the gathering crowd in the reception hall on the ground floor of the *Orbit* hotel and resort. The last of the rays of sunshine, like aged gold, pierced the immense glass windows behind Ralph and gave him a halo. *Ever a showman*, I thought to myself with a smile. He sat on a wooden stool, one leg on the floor, the other raised to hold up his guitar.

The scruffy beard that was his trademark was more salt than pepper these days and he tied his long, silver hair into a loose ponytail.

When we're old and bored and gray,
Will our love be enough?
When we've raged and changed and aged,
Will it all have been a bluff?

For you, my love, I'd die a thousand times or more...

My obsessive nature directed me to mildly tolerate the soppy lyrics while pulling the epic orchestration for *Seeds of Soulless* from my memory. The music flooded my ears and lifted my heart even though it wasn't really here.

My hand rested on Elle's hip as she swayed gently to the rhythm set by Ralph Nye's guitar. It was then that I noticed Dad walking through the crowd of pearly, polished guests. He stopped to greet most of the people along the way, all the while glancing at Elle and me.

My heart twisted in my chest and I forced my lungs to keep working steadily. Still, my palms quickly grew slick with cold sweat.

I hadn't seen him in weeks, which meant I also hadn't talked to him. He knew little of what I did when I wasn't with him and he asked less. His way of showing affection or keeping our relationship going was to keep my card loaded and to not freak out when I got sound systems or gaming stations or went on surprise trips. However, if he knew who I went with and why... Let's just say I wouldn't be surprised to find out that Dad always carried scissors with him to cut my card in half. I could already see him reaching into the inside pocket of his black evening jacket.

I had never lacked for anything in my life. It was a wonder I didn't turn into a spoiled brat because all I had ever needed to do was point. "I want it, Daddy, and I want it *now*," words from a movie echoed in my mind.

The crowd showered Ralph Nye with an ovation and he took a little bow, then spoke into the microphone about taking a short break. Once he was off the stage, the atmosphere seemed a little more relaxed as people mingled among themselves.

"I'll be right back," I whispered to Elle.

She nodded as I walked after the evening's entertainer. The man, the legend, sat at the bar with a martini just served to him.

"Uncle Ralph," I said as I walked up behind him. He wasn't my real uncle. Godfather felt too formal; Ralph felt too informal despite the years I'd known him.

"Ah, is that my favorite godson?" he asked in his booming, colorful voice. He gave a hearty laugh as he turned around and spread his arms.

I hugged him tightly. "I bet you say that to all your godchildren," I teased.

"You got me," he said and raised his hands in defense after we parted. "You've grown."

"I'm twenty-two," I pointed out.

"Consider reining it in, my boy," he said as I sat down on the barstool next to him and pointed to his glass for the waiter. Though I wasn't a fan of martinis or any beverages stronger than a normal beer, I enjoyed the man's company and quirks too much to resist it.

"I'll see what I can do about that," I said with a laugh. London liked my size quite a lot so I felt like

I had an incentive to buff up a little more. "Aren't you touring?" I asked.

Ralph Nye nodded. "I returned the day before yesterday," he explained. "Just in time to support Children's Hospital." He referred to the gala.

"I bet it was a roaring success," I said.

He waved his hand at me. "Stop with the flattery, Gabriel. How are you?"

I thought about this simple question. How was I? Normally, had anyone else in this entire hotel asked me that, I would nod curtly and say I was doing very well. But this was the man who had given me glimpses of life outside the norms of my father's rigid beliefs and rules. This was the man who cared little about the riches, though he had amassed plenty during his lifetime. This was the man who followed his muse wherever it took him and never really cared about anything else. The free-spirited artist who wasn't starving was very much the reason why I *didn't* end up a spoiled brat.

I'd seen him more often when I was a little child. But his career had taken a downturn, then, and he had had plenty of time for his godson.

"I, uh..." I shook my head. "I'm really good, Uncle Ralph. I'm really, really good."

His thick, white mustache sprinkled with a few dark gray hairs twitched and he allowed a bright smile to emerge. His eyes, pale blue, twinkled. "You very much seem so, dear boy."

I wanted to tell him everything. If anyone in the world would understand, it would be the man who had made a life of writing love songs in his unique folk-meets-rock style. The man who never had a marriage that lasted more than a year, yet who kept trying. The man who's lyrics, however cheesy to our generation, truly understood the mysteries of a human heart. "Pumping blood is only its pastime," Ralph Nye had once famously said to a crowd of ten thousand.

"Something's the matter," he said.

I wrinkled my nose and shook my head vehemently. "No, Uncle. It's not at all like that. I don't think I've ever been happier."

He gazed at me for a moment longer, then picked up the olive from his martini and bit a small chunk off. "If that is the case, say no more. Nobody needs to know."

Somehow, deep down, I felt like he knew. Not the details, of course, but the grand scheme of things. He knew the big picture of it all.

"Are you going to give us another song?" I asked in order to change the topic a little.

"I'm not here to juggle, Gabriel," he said mock-sternly, then cracked a smile under the thick mustache.

"Make it a happy one, Uncle," I said as I squeezed his shoulder.

"Just don't throw your bra on the stage," he joked. He'd always been critical of the sweeping fame of rock stars who had such audiences, but in the lovingly unique way of his.

I snorted at him and began asking questions about the tour. It was much more fun than the bruised hearts he usually talked about. And frankly, his anecdotes from touring were far more mild and PG-13 these days than they had been when I was, in fact, thirteen.

"Ralphie," the friendly growl came from behind and slicked my palms with new cold sweat. "Son," Dad said to me as a greeting.

"What's up, Dad?" I said over my shoulder, slightly annoyed that Uncle Ralph's story was interrupted, but more afraid of blurting out something stupid. *I'm going to top tonight*, for example.

Get out of my head, I hissed internally. Yet as soon as I was around someone who really wasn't supposed to know, these were the thoughts that intruded.

Dad grumbled under his pencil mustache and directed his attention to Uncle Ralph. He scanned my martini twice during the conversation. Each time, his face grew redder. He couldn't contain himself, so he turned to me in the end, and squeezed, "We will discuss this later."

And imagine if we were to discuss everything else that's going on, I thought and sighed internally. Instead of saying anything, I gave a curt nod. He didn't approve. He didn't approve of alcohol; he didn't approve of London hanging out with Elle and me; he didn't approve of games I played. That was his defining trait and the only trait I knew him for.

My father's disapproval was a fact of life. It was also the driving force behind my mother's choice to leave.

Once he was gone, Ralph Nye sighed and shook his head. His deep voice had a purr to it that made women swoon and men fidget with insecurities. "Your old man's regressing with years," he said sadly.

I tapped Uncle Ralph's shoulder as I got off the barstool. "Just make it a happy song, Uncle."

His chuckle followed me as I waded through the crowd of guests.

CHAPTER TWELVE

Mayhem Ensues

————— elle —————

I RUBBED THE BRIDGE of my nose and sighed.

"But she's just so beautiful," Zach whispered to me, leaning against the bar.

I swallowed a rising growl. He'd tried convincing me that Elle and I looked nothing alike and we were literally identical, save for the hair lengths. She never wore mascara, all the while people assumed I did. At best, she would put on lipstick, and even that was rare.

"But you're supposed to be my boyfriend," I said.

He chuckled. "C'mon, dude," he said skeptically. "I'm just a date. Nobody's even looking at me."

That much was true. Since Zach was for all practical purposes my date, nobody took him seriously. Nobody bothered to glance at him twice or,

God forbid, get to know him. It was an unspoken understanding between all my extended family members and their close friends that my dates only ever showed up once. Why use brain space to memorize a name that won't matter a week from now?

"Okay, but if someone happens to see you drooling after Elle, it'll get you noticed." I wasn't too invested in this argument, though. What I really wanted to do was drool after Gabriel, who was chatting with his Dad awkwardly all the while holding Elle around her waist. Gabriel seemed tired. He was shaking his head, dismissing something.

I checked the time on my phone, then tucked it into my pocket. There were still two solid hours before I could come up with an excuse and go to my room to wait for Gabriel.

I locked stares with Gabriel's dad by accident. Now that we were looking at each other, I pulled on my casual mask and decided to win the staring contest. He never liked me. It wasn't a big mystery; he just didn't like guys who liked guys. Or anyone ever at all.

My poor Gabriel, I thought. *He'll never break free*.

The frowning man looked away first and I pumped my fist in my imagination. *I win*.

I didn't mind sneaking around. I didn't mind keeping him a secret. After all, I was the guy who got His Highness, Mateo, and Joshua out of the dorm without alerting Mateo's guards so that they could have a sweet, secret date. I liked the thrill of hiding to an extent. But it wasn't the hiding part that bothered me. It was the hiding *forever* bit.

I took my phone out again and found my texts with Gabriel.

Me: Could you ask your dad to shave that mustache off? He looks like a Bond villain.

The next moment, as I smirked to myself, Gabriel lifted his phone and glanced at the screen. His shoulder shook and he swallowed a laugh, but didn't look my way.

Gabriel: I hate being ten paces away.

Though I'd known as much, reading the words on my screen made my heart fuzzy and warm. *Soon*, I thought.

I scanned the room for something to help me pass the time. It seemed as though the harder I tried to make the minutes move, the slower they budged. Finally, I spotted a million dollar smile on the far end of the reception room. Wearing a modern tux and with his cute boyfriend under his arm, Caleb was doing the same thing I was, looking for familiar faces. Unlike me, though, he was more than happy to stop by and chat. He was all the buzz in our circles, dropping out of a prestigious college and abandoning his father's business empire to pursue his dream of acting. It wasn't something you saw every day.

"Come on, boyfriend," I said. "Let's say hi to my friends."

"Yes, sweetie," Zach said. I didn't know what was worse; the fact that he'd called me a sweetie or the contrast such a term of endearment had against the rough and rugged appearance of my fake date.

I sighed and took his hand in mine for everyone to see. *Just push through tonight and tomorrow*, I told myself. *Then, nobody will see you or ask you anything till winter holidays*. And if I was very lucky, Gabriel and I would run away somewhere far for New Year's and not see our — mainly, his — families until summer vacation.

We pushed through the small, closed off groups of people eating various types of *hors d'oeuvre* from silver platters, sipping Prosecco, politely laughing, and tapping their checkbooks for the donations at the end of the evening.

Ralph Nye sang on the stage softly; a happy tune for once. The guy was a downer most of the time with lyrics hard-focused on missed chances and the ones that got away.

I snatched Caleb's shoulder while he was looking away and shook him gently. "You are a sight for sore eyes," I said.

"You are a mine of cliches," he retorted as he spun his head and showered me with his Hollywood smile.

"Did that feel good?" I asked.

"Messing with you always feels good, London," he said and laughed out loud.

"Remind me again why I'm friends with you," I said sourly, then shook my head. "This is Zach. My date."

Caleb shook Zach's hand with a raised eyebrow while Jayden, Caleb's feisty soulmate, chuckled.

"What?" I asked.

"Nothing," Jayden said quickly. "It's just... Nothing."

Caleb cracked a smile and bit his lip. "Nice to meet you, Zach. I'm sure we'll be seeing a lot more of you."

Jayden laughed out loud.

"You know," I said with a sigh. "That fucker."

"What?" Caleb played dumb, but gave it away immediately. "Hudson told us nothing."

I shot him a look of 'you don't say' and dropped Zach's left hand from my right. "It's alright, dude," I told him. "They know." Then, I sent a penetrating gaze at the cheerful couple. "Don't say a word to anyone."

Caleb's shoulders relaxed a little. "Mum's the word."

"Who's a cliche mine now?" I teased. And while Hudson apparently couldn't keep a secret if his life depended on it — which it totally fucking did because I was going to kill him — I could still trust Caleb and Jayden and all of my friends. But outing Gabriel, even in a safe space, didn't sit well with me. *I'll talk to him tonight*, I decided internally.

"I see the party's going nicely," Caleb said as if to change the topic.

"Why are you even here?" I asked. My parents invited most of my friends, but didn't truly expect them to come. Their families, however, were expected.

"I can't miss a show," Caleb said.

"Let's just hope there's no show here tonight," I said, tired by now.

Jayden nudged Caleb with his elbow and smiled.

"It's Gramps, actually," Caleb explained with a smile that matched his boyfriend's. "He never misses a fundraiser if he's invited, but all my aunts, who usually join him, are vacationing together in Malta."

"He didn't ask," added Jayden. "But we knew he didn't want to go alone."

"And so, we had to listen to him retell the entire plot of the *Twilight* saga in the car," Caleb said with a shudder.

"Gramps is team Edward, in case you're wondering," Jayden said with a playful eye-roll.

Caleb glanced around, then pulled Jayden's hand. "We better check in on him before he starts a book club, babe."

And with that, the two love birds flew away, leaving me with my lovely fake date to keep me entertained the rest of the evening.

When I turned the old fashioned key in the lock of my door and pushed it ajar, I found that a lamp was on inside my room. I sure hadn't left it on. My heart tripped and butterflies took wing in my stomach as I slipped inside without opening the door all the way, then shut it and leaned against it.

The sound of water coming from the bathroom lasted a few moments, then was off.

The room was an apartment, in fact, with a short hallway leading into the small living room. There, we had a balcony overlooking the resort and the open ocean beyond it. And on the left side of the living room was an open door leading to the bedroom, where the bathroom was attached.

Gabriel hummed one of Ralph Nye's songs once he turned the water off and I thought it was the most adorable thing in the world. God forbid I ever told him so; he would never stop humming. But he was such a sweet dork that my vision was coated with pink and I wanted to kiss every inch of his sculpted body.

I had conclusive evidence, at last. An entire day without Gabriel was a day wasted.

The bathroom door flew open and steam flavored with lavender came first. Then, wet haired but fully dressed in a loose T-shirt and a pair of knee-length shorts, walked out Gabriel. His bare arm was bent and his biceps tense as he rubbed his hair with a towel.

"Hey gorgeous," I whispered, unable to stop myself. "Getting comfortable?"

He grinned at me, threw the towel onto the sofa, and rushed across the room. His arms were wrapped around me in an instant, holding me tightly, as he pressed his lips hard against mine.

I turned to a puddle of feelings as I kissed him back.

Then, Gabriel pulled his head away and gazed into my eyes. As if I could be more in love with him than I had already been, I felt the heat rise to my cheeks. "I've been waiting the whole day for this," he said.

Sure enough, the last time I'd kissed him had been this morning.

All I could do was smile in reply. But he didn't wait for words to come. Instead, he clutched me tighter and kissed me harder, moving us both back toward the door. And when he pinned me against it, my breaths grew quick and I wanted nothing more than to let him have his way with me. It would be a fun change of roles we played when we were alone.

"Wait," I whispered, the fact that I'd told Hudson about him was still troubling me. "Wait, I need to tell you something."

Gabriel kissed my neck hungrily. "You can talk," he murmured between the kisses.

I chuckled and slapped his broad back gently. "No, no, we'll do this after."

He laughed into my neck, sending the vibration of his voice through my entire body.

As Gabriel stepped back, I took his hand in mine, tangled our fingers, and led him around to the sofa. We sat facing each other and I couldn't ignore the lustful look he was giving me. "That shirt looks so good on you," he said in his low purr. "And the bow-tie? Don't get me started on that."

I was not a fan of dress codes at these gatherings, but if Gabriel liked me in this, I would never wear anything else. But first, I needed to tell him everything.

I played with his fingers in my hand. "Can I tell you something?" I began, cussing internally at how badly that sounded.

"Sure," Gabriel said, unsuspecting.

"But, please don't freak out," I said and bit my lip, then met his gaze.

He toned down his playful expression, but it wasn't quite gone from his eyes. "What happened?" he asked.

Guilt soared in me; it scorched the trail as it climbed from my stomach to my throat. "I... I was talking to Hudson and he figured out I was, um..." *Serious with a guy? In love? Practically ready to settle down?* None of those were ideal ways to put it. "Dating," I said. "Someone."

"Uh-huh," he said carefully, not pulling his hand away. An eyebrow arched and he kept looking at me.

"I told him," I admitted. "About you."

Gabriel nodded. "Okay?"

"And he told Caleb," I said, guilt still growing denser.

"And?" Gabriel asked suspiciously.

"Um... And nothing," I said. "That's it. My friends know. He swore he wouldn't, but he let it slip. It's my fault. I should have known. He's not malicious or anything, he's just a naive loud-mouth."

Gabriel chuckled.

"But they know," I added. "And probably more of them know."

A wrinkle emerged on his forehead as he gave it some thought. Then, he nodded. "And that's a problem?"

I frowned. "Well, yeah. I outed you without your consent. That's not cool. I'm sorry."

Gabriel narrowed his eyes and thought about it for a few more moments. No doubt his analytical brain was humming perfectly inside that beautiful head. Then, he met my gaze again, but his expression was that of confusion. "London, they were bound to find out sooner or later," he said.

The knot in my throat loosened, untied fully, and dissolved. "You're not mad?"

He shook his head vehemently. "Why would I be mad? They're your friends."

"But you're still..."

Gabriel raised his other hand and waved it to stop me right there. "Look, they're all gay, right? It's not like they're gonna taunt me or out me to my dad." He sighed. "That was the only thing stopping me from taking you for a goddamn dance down there."

I chuckled. "To Ralph's music? Doubt it."

He laughed. "Fair enough." After our laughter died down, he took a slow, deep breath of air. "He'll find out soon enough. But..."

"I know," I said.

"It won't be nice," Gabriel said grimly. With a resigned voice, he continued. "I know it'll be the day I lose the last of my family."

I can be your family, I thought. Instead of saying anything, I simply nodded, and Gabriel tightened his hold on my hand.

"And I'm not ready to do that," he said. "I know, it's inevitable. It'll happen. Sooner or later, he will find out and I don't mean to live in hiding forever, but... How do you choose the right moment? How do you think, 'Now's the time to sever all the bonds?'"

I shook my head. "I don't know." Because I couldn't know. I couldn't possibly imagine the weight of it. When would it ever be the right time?

"Yeah," he whispered.

I looked into his eyes. I couldn't answer any of the questions. I couldn't help him choose the time. But I could close my hands around his face and lean in. And that is exactly what I did. We were an inch away from a kiss when a horrified, bone-chilling voice boomed through the door.

"What on Earth are you doing? What is the meaning of this?!" The voice snapped the last word with disgust and my heart twisted.

"Dad," Gabriel whispered.

"Crap," I said, voice frail and weak. Chills rushed down my spine as I shot off the sofa and headed for the door.

"London," Gabriel called pleadingly, as if knowing our dream was to end with me opening the door. But I knew, in my heart, what the hell was going on.

"It's not what it looks like," Elle pleaded in the hallway.

"It's most certainly exactly what it looks like you little minx," the vicious, spiteful voice boomed.

"London," Gabriel whispered in a last ditch effort to pretend nothing was happening. Because if I opened this door, I would get involved. He would have no choice. The moment was here too soon; and it was now.

My heart sank lower as I wrapped my hand around the knob. She was in trouble. I'd tear the world down to get her out of trouble. She'd made my dream come true, even if it lasted a short while; I had to step in.

The door flew open and the red face with a pencil mustache was sneering at my sister.

Gabriel's footsteps rushed across our room and he stood behind me. Silent.

"Call my sister that one more time, I fucking dare you," I growled at the man.

Zach, *my date*, stood confused and with messy hair, shoulder to shoulder with Elle. *Fuck*, I thought. *They were doing something when this guy walked in.* They were both dressed, so I could only hope they'd been making out and nothing more.

"I was looking for my son," the man said. "Only to find this...this..." He slurred the words and pursed his lips, his pencil mustache twitching at the ends. "You brought this down on us." He snapped his hate-filled look from me to Zach. The corners of his lips were wet with spit.

"Dad," Gabriel said.

My heart jumped. If there ever was a right time, it was now, forced as if might have been.

"No," Elle said. She shot a look to Gabriel. "I'm sorry, Gabriel. I don't love you anymore."

My mouth went dry and I balled my fists.

"What nonsense is this?" this asshole asked of his son, then cocked his head at Elle.

Do it. Do it, now, I thought.

But Gabriel was silent.

Elle wasn't. She wrung her hands together and took the bullet. "I'm sorry it had to happen like this. I didn't mean to hurt you."

I sent a furious look to Gabriel, who opened his mouth, then closed it. His eyes were shining and he was shaking his head in tiny, jerky moves.

"Gabriel," I whispered.

"Stay out of this," his dad snapped. "You brought this young man here." He refused to look at Zach while Zach bared his teeth at the man.

"Stephen," I tried pleading. "You don't know..." I swallowed the rest, but he was quick, too.

"Stay. Away." His growl was a deep rumble.

I looked at Gabriel again at the same time his father did. *Come on, you coward. Now's the time. She took the fucking bullet for you.*

"This family has embarrassed us enough, Gabriel. Forget about her."

"I'm sorry," Elle mouthed, still pretending to be the villain here just to...do what? Ensure that Gabriel and his dad didn't fall out? Who fucking cared?

Not for once did this blindfolded asshole think why Gabriel was in my room while Elle was with my supposed date. Not once did he think to question it. He was so far lost in his denial that he could only see Elle for a cheater and Gabriel for a victim.

I was breathing furiously and waiting for one of them to solve this dilemma, but nobody did. Elle buried her face in her hands and started to cry and I had no fucking clue if she was really crying or pretending for theatrics' sake.

Gabriel's eyes shone with pooling tears. He knew he could have stopped the bully if he had the balls, but he didn't lift a finger. He knew I was watching.

We all made choices in this moment.

Zach wrapped his arms around Elle and looked at me with a sad shake of his head. His role as my date was quickly fading away and he didn't care. He was holding the person he adored.

Nobody could say as much about Gabriel or me. We held no one.

"Gabriel, we are leaving," Stephen snapped. "This charade has gone on for too long. Forget about her. She's not worth it."

I tightened my fist, ready to dislodge the fucker's jaw.

Gabriel did nothing.

He said nothing.

He looked at the floor.

"Gabriel," I whispered.

His father stormed the fuck off down the hallway.

"Gabriel," I said again.

He didn't move.

Zach turned Elle around and wrapped his arms around her fully. She rested her head on his shoulder, face pressed against his neck.

Rage boiled in my stomach and I spun around, stormed back inside the room, and shut the door.

CHAPTER THIRTEEN

Paying the Price

—ele—

DAD'S POISONOUS STARE LEFT its sting on me long after he was gone from sight.

I couldn't force my feet to move even after Zach pulled Elle toward their room.

The only thing I could do was croak, "Elle. I'm sorry."

She paused and let go of Zach, then threw her arms around me. "Don't be," she whispered. "You're still safe."

But is it worth it? Is it worth the rage you received and the talk that will break out in a minute? I had no doubt about Dad marching up to Mr. and Mrs. Reynolds and telling them everything down to the last detail, as well as everyone else he saw on his way there.

"You shouldn't have saved me," I whispered back.

"Shh." It was all she said before letting go and walking inside her room where Zach was waiting. He had anger flashed in his eyes when he looked at me and shut the door.

With a heavy heart and a heavier stride, I turned around and walked into London's room.

He was sitting in the armchair in the living room, his back facing the hallway and me. He wasn't looking out the window across the room. Instead, his head was hanging and he was staring at the floor.

"London," I said. Again, my tongue was tied and I barely managed as much. Afterwards, I was silent. Moment by moment, step by step, I neared him until I was just a couple of paces away.

Guilt twisted my insides with its cold, steely grip.

"Remember when you said how hard it was to find the right time?" London's voice had gone cold and emotionless. It was cutting with its crisp edge.

I held my breath.

"That was it," he said without looking.

I opened my mouth, but then closed it. No matter what, I couldn't find the words that would make a difference. I'd fucked up hard this time.

London twisted in the armchair but still didn't look at me. "She's getting the full blow of that asshole's rage today," he said, his voice still without a memory of warmth.

"I'm sorry," I said.

"Oh, all good, then." London clapped his hands joyfully and spun around with a big grin on his face. It sliced through my soul. The grin dissolved and turned to a bitterness-filled sneer. "I get it," he said, softening the edge of his words and the sarcasm. "And I don't need you to come out; I really don't. Not for me. I don't need you to admit it to anyone, ever, if you don't want to. Have me, keep me a secret, take me away. But don't let *her* pay the price."

My eyebrows trembled and vision blurred. He still wanted me to have him, to keep him, to take him away.

"You couldn't stand up for her," he said. "And that's my problem, Gabriel. When push comes to shove, are you going to be there?"

I sucked in my lower lip and closed my teeth around it, fighting my muscles to stay still and stop shaking.

"Or are you going to let everyone else take the fall?" He scoffed and shook his head, then shot to his feet and walked around the room. "You didn't dare speak up because it would raise questions, huh? But where's the line? Where's the fucking line?" He ran his slender fingers through his rich, brunette hair. "He's going to tell everyone how you're the victim here. He's going to be the right-eous asshole he's always been."

Every word he said was true.

My father was no father. He was a man obsessed with how he was seen in his own world.

"And what then? He'll remove the limit off your card to help you feel better. I know this, Gabriel. I know this because I've watched you from afar my entire life. I've seen every move you've ever made, but I thought you were better than him. I thought..." He covered his face with both his hands and tilted his head back. "It's family," he murmured. "It's family and it's not easy to give up on him, I get it."

My heart cracked and broke for the debate I made him have with himself. Every word he said was a small contradiction as he looked over the entire situation.

"I..." My voice choked and I cleared my throat. "I want to make it better. I want to fix this."

"You better," he said and dropped his arms by his sides.

Slowly, he stepped once, twice, thrice, and stood in front of me. His face was tense and lips pursed, but his eyes wore all the hurt of this world.

"London, I'm sorry," I said again for the lack of anything else. How was I going to fix this? "Please... Just don't..." I couldn't even say the words. *Don't leave me.*

His eyes shone with unshed tears. He simply shook his head as if to say he didn't know what to do. "Can you even fix it?" he asked after a moment of silence.

"I can try," I promised. "If you're with me, I can..."

He closed his eyes, eyelashes wet, and turned his head away from me. His hand rose near my chest but never touched me. It lingered in the air until he moved past me. "I need to get out of here."

Quietly, he slipped away and left me alone to stew in my bitterness and blunder.

I stood in silence as the door opened and shut and a faded, faraway knock on Elle's door reached me. Hushed voices came through, but I couldn't make out the words. Instead, I let everything melt away and closed my eyes. I didn't know how long I was standing there. It felt like ages passed and eras turned.

There was only one way out of this. There was only one way to protect Elle from mean and vicious gossip. There was only one way to prove to London where my loyalty lay.

But London's disappointment in me ran deep. It hurt in places I hadn't known could feel pain.

So I tightened my fists and turned on my heels. My entire life, I had been given everything so long as I played by the rules. The rules were simple; all I had to do was tick the boxes for what my father's son should be. A valedictorian, so he could brag at parties; active in extracurricular, *so he could brag at parties*; have a girlfriend, so he could brag at fucking parties...

I stormed down the hallway, down the stairs, and up another hallway until I found his room. My knock was firm and short and I tried barging in, but it was locked.

My heart sank lower, but anger fueled its furious beating. Using the last drops of adrenaline my body could squeeze out, I descended another floor and pushed through the crowd where my father had cornered Mr. Reynolds.

"Frankly, Stephen, I don't see how this is any of my business," Mr. Reynolds was saying to my red-faced dad.

"Don't be ridiculous," Dad protested. "You approve of adultery."

"They are old enough to make their decisions. Obviously, we wouldn't approve, but this matter is not in our hands. Leave them to their devices. Let them make mistakes."

"Mistakes?" Dad was incredulous. "Mistakes?! Let me tell you what I..."

"Dad," I snapped as I reached the two men. "Stop this. Stop it, at once."

Anger flared in his eyes. "Stay out of this, Gabriel."

I let out a bitter, contemptuous chuckle. "Stay out of this? It's my life you're talking about." I shook my head and glanced around the room. My heart thumped ever faster. "It's *my* life and you don't have the slightest idea of what's going on." The resignation — the surrender and giving up on the idea of a family — creeped into my voice.

Dad's eyes narrowed. He must have gotten a hunch that this wasn't going to go his way. He didn't want to hear it.

"Mr. Reynolds, I apologize for this," I said. Ron shook his head in dismissal as if to say there was nothing to apologize for. He even opened his mouth, probably to console me in the light of the events upstairs. I raised my hand quickly. "It's not at all what my dad made it out to be. He wasn't there."

"Oh," Ron said in confusion.

"Gabriel, this is your last..." Dad tried, but I cut in.

"Stop harassing and bullying," I snapped, keeping my voice clipped and low so as not to make a scene in front of everyone. "If you ever bothered once in my whole life, you would know that this is not what I want. Who the fuck throws a tantrum this way?"

This was rubbing it in too much for Dad. Spittle gathered in the corners of his trembling lips.

"Elle didn't cheat on me," I admitted. I was past the point of no return. It was either this or an eternity of playing to the tune of his fiddle. "Elle and Zach are together."

"What?" Ron Reynolds asked, his voice mostly surprised, but also a tiny bit amused. I wondered what he really thought of this. Would he disapprove? Or would he, once again, step up as a parent and welcome Zach the way he had welcomed me?

I nodded. "They're dating."

"Gabriel, you are in shock," Dad said.

I laughed. "And you are in denial." I could relate. I'd been in denial for too long. I'd been so far gone in denial that I hadn't realized how much I was in love with London until the moment I almost lost it. "Elle and I broke up and didn't tell anyone. We would have told you," I said as I turned to Ron, who definitely would have been the first on our list. Then I turned to my dad again. "The reason we told no one was because she was protecting me. The reason you're shouting here is because she's still protecting me." Despite my best efforts, my voice began to tremble and crack. And, as my vision blurred, I wanted to curse at myself for being so weak. *You can do this*, I whispered internally. *Rip it off quickly and be done with it.*

"Protecting you from what?" Dad asked in a low growl, then shook his head. "I don't need to hear this. You are clearly..."

"I'm gay is what I am," I said, breathless. In the split second before the words had left me, I realized I wasn't ready. I also realized I never would be. There was no time or place or alternative universe in which this would have been easy and in which the moment would have been prepared for. London — my sweet, brave, perfect London — had gone to hell and back before coming out and his parents had never batted an eye at it.

Yeah. There was no easy way. There was only this way.

I shrugged at my dad's gaping mouth. "I'm gay. I'm dating someone. Elle offered to help me keep it a secret."

Ron Reynolds' lips moved into a fraction of a proud smile. 'That's my girl,' the smile said. He also took a step back, as if to allow for some privacy. But I noticed that he didn't move all the way back. He must have known how likely this was to escalate.

"You are not," Dad said briskly. "Gabriel, this will upset your mother."

I snorted. "You dare talk about my mother? What do you know? She escaped you and left me in your care. For all I care, she can be upset, but I fucking doubt it." A long, tired sigh dragged its way out of my chest. "I can't play this stupid game anymore. I can't hide in the closet while you're around. And I hope you're around for many happy years, I do, but I won't pretend until the day you're gone. I won't do it, Dad."

"Stop this nonsense, Gabriel," he said, his voice full of uncertainty. Did he seriously think it was a prank?

"Nonsense? I don't think so." I crossed my arms at my chest simply to stop my hands from shaking. Or, at least, to hide the shaking from Dad. "I have a boyfriend." *Maybe not for long. Maybe he quits on me. But I still goddamn have one and I love him.* The words ran through my head, but I didn't speak them. Instead, I said, "And you have to live with it one way or another."

"Stephen," Ron tried.

"This is none of your business, Reynolds," Dad barked. "It wouldn't surprise me if your family did this. All that time he was with that freak of yours..."

"Stephen, you should leave," Ron said firmly, not losing his composure.

"Take that back," I growled at Dad.

"...he filled his head with these ideas," Dad finished.

"Take that back," I said again but he kept ignoring me. Instead, he took a sudden step toward Ron, like he was about to trample him, and turned at the last moment before impact. Then, he marched the fuck out of the reception hall.

"I'm sorry," I whispered to Ron.

"Not your fault, kid. You're alright," Ron said with a nod. He wasn't a man of many words, but you could bet your ass his words were true to their core.

I wanted to apologize again, but I had to finish this business once and for all. So, I rushed after my dad.

"Hey," I called as I headed after him. "Hey!"

Dad stopped and turned on his heels, jaws clenching.

I spread out my arms. "Is this it? You're just gonna bury your head in the sand?"

"What do you want me to say, Gabriel?" he asked and closed his fists.

That you love me no matter what, I thought and almost laughed at it. As if. He'd never said it before. Why start now?

His eyes narrowed. "You knew what would happen, Son, and you made your choice."

"For one, I didn't choose to fall in love with a guy," I said as my arms dropped by my sides.

He shook his head. "You chose to tell me."

"You're right," I said with a jerky nod. "I expected nothing less. But I still hoped..." I choked on my words.

He shook his head to stop me right there. "Gabriel, let me make this very clear. I have given you everything you could possibly want. You have never, not once, lacked for anything. You have been brought up in privilege most cannot even dream of. And this is your way of thanking me. So be it. Consider your cards deactivated and your tuition payments halted. I will make an effort not to intrude, but you must make an equal effort not to cross my path again." And as if his cold, calculated tone was not enough, he added, "I have no son."

I swallowed the thick knot in my throat and nodded. What I lacked my whole life was beyond the comprehension of the man who had once called himself my father. I had lived without it for twenty-two years. I could very well live some more.

"It's a testament to what I lacked," I started slowly. "The fact I feel almost nothing in this moment."

Stephen nodded and turned away on his heels.

A bitter taste coated my tongue, but I forced myself to see reason. The price of freedom was steep until I saw how little he cared for the human in me and how much it had always been about appearances. I turned away from him and walked back into the hotel. The sting of being an outcast, even in the eyes of someone who had never bothered, seared my insides. But it wasn't supposed to. My stride had an air of lightness in it that hadn't been there before. By all means, I was free. What I lost only bore weight when all my fictitious ideas of a father and a son were piled onto it. What I truly lost, I had never had.

And when I walked back into the hotel, and when I left the man who had been my father outside, the twisting in my stomach passed and I took a deep breath of air.

It was over.

CHAPTER FOURTEEN

The Sole Prize

———eee———

I SWIRLED THE STRAW in my cocktail and growled whenever anyone neared either of the barstools around me. The bartender knew better than to ask.

Ralph Nye insisted on his sappiest songs to my eternal delight. They struck the chord of what I felt in this very moment.

Decisions, decisions, I thought without actually attempting to make one.

The pitiful glances that came my way made me want to bark, but I settled for low growls in my throat and cocktail sipping. They pitied me for the shame my family faced and it wasn't fair. *Oh, poor London to have to see that. Poor Ron and Judy. At their very own gala*, the pearl-clutching, cocktail dress-wearing ladies and fine-combed, tux-clad gentlemen thought when they saw me.

After leaving Gabriel to think or act or whatever he'd had to do, I had knocked on Elle's door. She seemed perfectly fine to me, except for deciding to stay in the room and sneak out in the morning. "I'll talk to Mom and Dad before I leave," she had told me. "Just... Don't blame him. It's not his fault."

It wasn't. Yet I couldn't convince myself that Gabriel hadn't had the chance to stop it.

What am I going to do with you? I wondered.

I'd never been one who needed proof of love. Never before had my entire life depended on a guy looking into my eyes and telling me, once and for all, that all he wanted was me. But right now, I saw no way forward without exactly that. Just like all the hidden romance novels under my bed promised always happened, I sat at the bar and waited. I waited knowing full well that the likelihood of that happening was null.

Real life wasn't as romantic or as kind as it was in stories. It seemed to me I had to learn that the hard way.

Sheer instinct made me turn my back around and glance over my shoulder. A pair of green-brown eyes was on me in an instant when Gabriel stopped walking through the crowd. His gaze asked a question for which I had no answer.

I licked my lips and watched him.

His eyebrows rose a little, then fell into a determined frown, and Gabriel marched across the reception hall to the small stage where Ralph was just wrapping up his *Ballad of A Thousand Loves*.

Gabriel tapped his godfather's shoulder and whispered in his ear, received a firm nod, and stood straight.

"That will be it for now, folks," Ralph Nye said in his booming, whiskey voice. "But I will leave you with my godson, who has a few words to share." He mouthed something to Gabriel away from the microphone.

Gabriel unhooked the microphone with a shaking hand and my heart twisted. What the hell was he about to do?

I stilled my feet on the lower bar of my barstool and forced myself to stay put. If I didn't put my muscles to work, I would rush after him and drag him off that stage. But the look of determination on his face left me sitting.

Gabriel lifted the microphone and cleared his throat loudly. "Sorry," he murmured. "Ah, sorry, everyone. I'm, ah, about to make a fool of myself, maybe. If you'd all just give me a minute of your time..." The room fell completely quiet and I wanted to drop through the ground. "My father wasted no time. Just as I walked through here, I heard Elle's name mentioned three times and I cannot — *cannot* — let this go on for another minute." Gabriel closed his eyes for a moment and scratched the back of his head with his free hand. He sighed. "He really wanted everyone to hear about it. He thrives on being the one who was wronged."

A murmur passed through the crowd.

"No, no. Don't pretend it's not true. We all know him; some know him better, others are more fortunate."

An awkward chuckle trembled through everyone.

Gabriel shook his head. "The truth is, he's really giving it his best to get that coveted martyrdom and this was too good a chance to pass on. Except, it's a lie." He scoffed. "My father didn't lie, though. He is incapable of telling you a lie. But he was mistaken and lied to and I'm sure he wishes it was still so."

Get off that stage, I whispered internally. *You don't have to do this*. But didn't he? I wasn't sure.

"It's not fair that Elle should pay the price," Gabriel said. "When I'm the one who caused this mess. See, she cheated on no one. We broke up. A while ago, in fact. And all she did was to protect me from gossip and my father's wrath. But, since I'm taking away all the juicy stuff we all could have talked about, I'll also give you some back." He took a deep breath of air. "Most of you have known me my entire life. Most of you expected Elle and me to get married any time now. I'm not particularly sad to say that we won't be doing anything close to it. She's my best friend and really the only girl I ever loved. But the problem is, I don't love girls. It took me a lifetime to figure that out, but I'm not even close to being straight." He chuckled like a madman. "Phew, it's much easier the second time around. Ah, my dad decided he no longer has a son, by the way." His voice echoed through a still and silent room and a few gasps sounded. "Right," Gabriel said. "I knew I'd lose what's left of my family once I came out. It's okay." He paused and looked around, his gaze finding mine. "I just needed you all to know that Elle played along so that *this* wouldn't happen. And for that, we all owe her a world of love and gratitude; me, most of all." He paused again and swallowed. He was about to break. His free hand rubbed the T-shirt he was wearing as if he was wiping the cold sweat away. "I don't expect anyone will see much of my father. Especially not today. In case you couldn't tell by the lack of tension in the room, he left a few minutes ago. But here's the thing. I'm fine with that. I see worried faces around here, chest-holding and all. Don't be worried. I really am fine because it took me a big, scary leap to realize that family isn't a fixed construct. It couldn't be further from it. So, um..."

And then, his gaze locked onto mine. The pull was so strong that I stood up and clutched the edge of the bar so I wouldn't swoon all the way down to the floor.

"...London, you were right. The moment was there and I missed it. I hope... I hope this begins to fix the mess I made."

We made, I thought.

"And I hope you know that you've always been all the family I needed or wanted. I..." He took a shallow breath of air as the room moved around me and I found myself nearing the stage. "I love you, London."

I didn't know when the stage crossed the room to me. I didn't know when the crowd collectively parted and the universe folded in on itself for this quantum leap that took place. All I knew was that I found myself on the stage and a foot away from Gabriel.

He was looking into my eyes and the microphone sent a screeching sound that ripped everyone's ears when it dropped against the floor. But I was deaf to it all. My hand clutched Gabriel's T-shirt and I was pulling him in.

His lips smashed against mine and I kissed him like our lives depended on it. The murmur around us grew into a thunder and someone began to speak loudly in a booming, whiskey voice, then sounding a chord on the guitar.

But I heard none of it. Not really. The applause passed through me, never quite sinking into my mind. The only thing that sank into my heart and soul and mind was the heat of Gabriel's kiss, the size of his body against mine, and the saltiness of our mingling tears. Were they happy? Were they sad? I had the rest of my life to figure that out.

CHAPTER FIFTEEN

For Better or Worse

———— ℓℓℓ ————

RALPH NYE GRABBED MY shoulder and gave a firm squeeze, but it came and went before I realized what was happening. His guitar sounded with an A Major chord, then a C Major. He was giving me a happy one.

"I love you," I murmured when my brow touched London's and our lips parted.

"You really do," London confirmed, his voice shaky and hushed.

"I really do," I echoed.

"And guess what?" he whispered. "I love you, too."

Flickers surged through my body and turned my heart to twice its size. It pounded in my throat, my head, my chest. Its pumping flooded my ears.

"And I'll be your family," he said. "Always."

My hands closed around his face as happy tears dampened my eyelashes.

"There you have it, folks," Ralph said softly into the microphone while his nimble fingers played the guitar. "Young love is messy, but it always wins."

"We better get off this stage unless you plan to do a striptease," London huffed and chuckled.

"Yeah, you might be right," I said and found his hand. As we took our first step as an official, public couple, I glanced at Uncle Ralph, who was taking in a breath of air and striking the note just right. The upbeat rhythm followed us down the steps off the stage and Uncle Ralph sent me a proud, fatherly smile. *My family is bigger than I ever imagined*, I thought as my gaze darted to the smiling crowd. The little stabs at their gossiping went unnoticed, I realized to my relief. They weren't offended. Or, if they were, they put it on hold to give me my moment.

"Dad," London said as he pulled me by my hand. "Meet Gabriel," he added with a warm chuckle. "My boyfriend."

Ron laughed out loud. "I think we've met each other." He opened his arms and took me in. It was more affection than I was used to, but I handled it without falling apart and crying on the man's shoulder.

Judy Reynolds was a pace behind and she hugged me next. "You're always going to have a family here, Gabriel," she said softly as her arms tightened around me.

"I'm so sorry," I said to them both. "I'm so sorry about..."

They both waved their hands to stop me. Judy said, "You did everything right."

"He really did, didn't he?" London added. "And now, if you'll excuse us, we are going to disappear."

"Disappear where?" Ron asked.

London smirked and my cheeks heated. "I think we all had enough of this crowd," London said. "Besides, I've got a test to get ready for. Can you just have Bradley bring the car around?"

Ron scoffed in a fatherly fashion, as if to say, 'I don't get you, kids,' but he didn't say no. Instead, he took out his phone.

London grabbed my hand and pulled me away before I had a chance to ask what the hell he was doing. Were we heading back to Santa Barbara? But he dragged me through the throng of richly dressed, smiling people until we were by the grand staircase near the exit.

"Get our stuff," he said and squeezed my hand. "I can't do half the things I want to do to you while everyone's watching."

I chortled, my cheeks aflame. "What do you have on your mind?"

London faced me and grinned. "Oh, my love," he said softly. "You really should know by now." Then, he let go of my hand and spun away, heading for the exit. He briefly turned his head over his shoulder. "I'm waiting outside."

My heart tripped and the mystery and excitement sent me running up the stairs. But when I reached the second floor — admittedly, a little out of breath — I didn't run into our room to get our things. Instead, I paused in front of Elle's.

My heartbeat slowed to normal and my breaths were deep and steady again. So, I knocked on her door.

She opened the door cautiously, then allowed a half-smile when she saw me.

"I came to say thank you."

"Good. I'd smack you if you apologized again." Elle grinned and swept a hand over her face, moving a lock of hair. *I love London so fucking much*, I thought, her gesture sparking his image into existence. He was waiting for me, taking me somewhere I was supposed to know by now.

"And I wanted to say that it's all good now," I added. "The air's clear."

"What do you mean?" Her brow wrinkled.

"I told my dad," I said.

"Gabriel..." It was a sigh.

I shrugged. "Don't really have a dad anymore, but we all knew it was just a matter of time."

She pushed out of the room and wrapped her arms around my neck.

"I'm fine," I added quickly. And, when she let go, I said, "It's like losing something you never really had. It's more about the idea than the reality. But I've got the biggest family I could hope for; in you, in London, your folks, Uncle Ralph... Hell, everyone down there swooned when I came out."

"You did what?" Elle's eyebrows shot up.

"You'll hear all about it when you join the party. And you really should. I told them everything."

Her cheeks turned a little pink and she chuckled. "And you and London?"

"I'm not sure. We're either eloping together or he's about to drop me in the middle of nowhere for embarrassing the crap out of him down there." I laughed. "Nah, we're good. Never better now that it's all over."

Elle was quiet for a little while. Her smile dimmed as she examined me. "I'm sorry about your dad, Gabriel."

"Don't be." There was nothing else I could say on that. He'd made his choice in a way that felt like he'd been waiting for that opportunity. "If it wasn't now, it would have been tomorrow; or in a month; or a year." It had been a ticking bomb either way.

"Just know that we all love you," she said.

And, for the first time, I truly felt it. It wasn't the thrilling, epic kind of love I felt after hearing London say it. It was much more somber and home-like. They did love me. "And I love you, too," I said. "Now, I gotta go before London starts a search party."

"Always partying, that one," Elle said with a sarcastic, over the top eye roll. She hugged me again, kissed my cheek, and ran her fingers down my neck before letting go. "See you soon."

Elle returned to her room and I walked into London's. My backpack was nearly fully packed. I threw in the stuff I'd worn at the start of the party, zipped it up, grabbed London's never unpacked, tiny suitcase, and headed out.

I was glad to leave *Orbit* behind me when I walked out the main doors and found London with his hands tucked in the pockets of his fitted, black pants. The white shirt was unbuttoned at the top and he'd taken off the bow-tie. He ruffled his sexy, light brunette hair, and looked like the London I knew and loved.

He half-smiled when he saw me and took two steps backward, nearing the car.

Bradley got out from behind the wheel as the trunk slowly opened. He greeted me and helped with the luggage as London and I got inside. The visor was up and I heard the faint sound of the driver's door open and close and we began moving.

"I didn't want it to go this way," London said.

I sighed. "There was no other way, London. It was always going to be like this."

"You're a braver man than I am," he said.

I shook my head. "When it came down to it, it wasn't so hard. I guess anger trumps fear."

"I can see that," he said with an understanding nod. "What now, though? Do you think he'll come around?"

"The ball is in his court," I said. "I won't ignore him if he tries, but... I don't think he will."

"Prick," London murmured and we laughed.

"There's something else," I said awkwardly. There was no easy way of saying this. "I'm officially broke." I tried softening it with a chuckle, but it only sounded worse. "Money's always been his way of expressing love, so that's pretty much done with. I... I have to tell you before...we..." He had to know, but it was far from easy.

London raised his eyebrows and gave a long sigh. "Oh well. I'll stop the car and we can go our separate ways, then."

I tried swallowing, but the lump in my throat grew.

And then, the fucker laughed. "You dumb-dumb," he said. "Why would you *have to* tell me? I mean, sharing is caring, but it's not like it matters to me."

"Wh... What?"

"I'm sorry he cut you off, but you knew it would happen," London said with a shrug. "We'll have to adjust."

We, he said.

"It's not like my family's gonna leave you hanging. We're together, beau. You and me."

Crap. I was going to cry. *Don't cry. Don't cry. Just don't cry.* I shook my head. "No way. I'm not gonna..."

"You're not gonna be stupid proud and refuse help to get back at your feet, mister. Besides, I happen to have a bunch of friends who care more about partying and hooking up than about their exams. I'll get you work in no time." He grinned. "We just gave to get me to pass first and I'll be a walking ad for your brand new tutoring gig."

I began laughing for no apparent reason. A mix of relief and joy of being around him boiled in me and began bubbling out of me. I grabbed his shirt where the first button was still holding it together, pulled him ruthlessly to me, and pressed my lips hard against his.

When the kiss passed a few moments later, London fanned his face. "Save that for later. We'll be there in half an hour."

"Be where?" I asked at last.

"You're cute," he answered. "Don't you know already?"

I shook my head at the mystery.

London smiled without a trace of his signature sarcasm. "It's the place where I fell in love with you twice as hard. Do you really think a night in that cabin was enough?"

My heart nearly exploded in my chest. The colorful, private little cabin, with its large bed up in the loft, and thick curtains to make us forget whether it was day or night, was easily the place I associated most with true happiness. It was the place where I knew, deep down, that he was nothing short of my soulmate.

Forever and ever and ever...

Chapter Sixteen

Only Yours

—ell—

It was my lucky day.

While waiting for Gabriel outside the hotel, I scored a short-notice reservation for the exact same cabin we'd been in not too long ago. Except, this time, we had three nights we otherwise would have spent being cute at my parents' gala.

Bradley dropped us off right in front of the cabin and I wasted no time in looking around or getting awestruck by the setting. Yeah, yeah, pretty trees and bushes and little birds. Whatever. I had Gabriel's hand in mine, my other hand on the small suitcase, and I was marching up the narrow path to the entrance door.

Gabriel, who was holding the key, unlocked the door. We pushed inside, shutting the door behind us and locking it. Enjoying the camp could come later. Now, all I wanted to enjoy was Gabriel.

"Should I get the hot tub going?" Gabriel asked as he dropped his backpack to the floor.

"Nah. You should be kissing me. We can dip in later." I took him by his hips and spun us around.

"You haven't swam in days," Gabriel said with over the top concern for me.

"I'm thinking I'm less of a fish and more of a sexy merman," I joked. My black eyebrows, manicured before the gala, wiggled at Gabriel as I pinned him against the door. "You're not getting rid of me that easily, sir."

"Sir," he echoed. "I like it."

I chuckled shortly. "How much do you like it?" My crotch pushed against him and I discovered just how much he liked it. "Oh. That much?"

To my surprise, Gabriel didn't blush or stammer. Instead, he let a purr rise from his chest and throat, eyes flashing with lust against the dim lamplights inside the cabin. His hands rested on the small of my back and he gave a little push.

Squeezing closer to him was never a bad thing. "I've been dying for this," I whispered, then caught a breath of air. His hands usually went up my back. Tonight, they went down. He cupped my ass freely, greedily. The entire week had gone by in an instant and, though we'd seen each other, we'd had no fun at all. Not like this, at least. Study, study, study; that was all we'd been doing lately. And it wasn't even close to the fun and sexy kind of studying we'd done in this very room last weekend.

Gabriel squeezed my butt harder and tingles ran down my arms. He let his head rest against the door while I planted kisses up and down his neck. "You're so fucking sexy," I murmured into his neck, making him tense a little.

When he made his hips dance slowly back and forth, left and right, each contact of his crotch against mine reduced the oxygen levels in my lungs. I kept exhaling nervously, kissing and licking his neck as if my life depended on it.

My hands reached under his T-shirt and felt the soft bits above his hips. I dragged them around to feel the small of his back, then all the way up to his broad shoulders. His body was on fire; each touch burned my fingertips.

"Tell me you love me," I whispered, then bit the soft part of his ear gently. When I was with him, my teeth needed something soft to sink in. When I was with him, my toes were restless until I curled them and twisted them in every way I could. When I was with him...

"I didn't realize I could love anyone this much," he said.

Oh fuck, that was the best answer.

I pushed into him harder, as if grinding my body against his was some sort of a reward for making me feel this way. Well, it was, in a way.

Gabriel moaned as our bodies pressed together and I clawed at his upper back. I needed more of him. I wanted us to be closer still.

"And I don't even think...ah..." His sighs freaking killed me. "I don't think I love you half as much as I will tomorrow. And even then, not half as much as the day after."

Holy fuck. It's like he's reading from one of the novels stashed under my bed. "Tell me that again tomorrow," I said.

Gabriel moved swiftly, spinning us around in an instant. My back pressed against the door and his chest pushed into mine. His knee bumped into the door between my legs and his thigh rubbed against my fully hard cock.

Each moment that passed while Gabriel's leg rubbed against my crotch added pressure right onto my chest. Breathing felt obsolete. It felt like a distraction from the sole thing I needed to stay alive.

Gabriel's lips grazed mine. They were soft and wet and red from my rough kisses. He pecked my lips once again, shortly. He teased me and toyed with me. He edged me in the sweetest, most painful ways there were.

I let my hands drop to his waist and grabbed the edge of his T-shirt. In one sweeping move, Gabriel's arms shot up and I pulled his T-shirt off, then let it drop onto the floor. He was quick to find the first fastened button in the middle of my chest and started undoing them each in turn until he reached my waist. The polished black belt was off in an instant.

While I let my hands worship his chest and arms and back, Gabriel undid the button on my pants, unzipped them, and let them drop around my ankles. He took my shirt off next, breaking the contact between my fingertips and his hardening nipples for a little while.

It was the perfect opportunity, so I used this moment to hook my fingers inside his shorts and pull them down as I dropped onto my knees. It was a fun twist to be the one kneeling, looking up pleadingly, waiting to feast on his body.

His dick was packed hard and tightly inside his boxer-briefs and I pressed my lips against the outline of his cock. It pulsed twice, quickly, as I dragged my lips over the soft and stretched fabric, then closed them around the tip. A moment later, when I pulled back, a wet stain showed on the dark blue textile and I wondered whether it was my saliva or his precum or both. Whichever was the correct answer, I quickly stopped caring, because Gabriel pushed his thumbs inside the waistband of his underwear and pulled them over his throbbing dick.

My mouth watered and I quickly licked my lips, worked some spit into my mouth, and glanced at him as my fingers wrapped around the base of his cock. He shuddered and gazed back at me as I opened my mouth for him.

The first move of his body was gentle and slow. The tip of his cock touched my open lips, rested on my tongue, and eased in gracefully. Gabriel's left hand ran over my head and took a fistful of my hair at the back.

Within a heartbeat, the roles were clear.

I sealed my lips around his dick and let him do the work. His grip on my hair never hurt for a second, but it was firm enough to hold me just the way I was. His hips swung forth, cock sliding in and pressing against my throat.

Tears filled my eyes after three such moves. Gabriel shoved himself a little harder this time, then held fast. I stopped breathing completely and watched him, looking helpless no doubt, as he winced and held it in for a moment longer.

When he pulled his big, hard cock all the way out, I slurped up the saliva that was trickling from the corners of my mouth, and quickly reached for another taste.

"Fuck, that's hot," Gabriel grunted as he eased himself back in.

I was so fucking ready for it, this time. I forced my throat to relax and open as Gabriel pushed himself in from above, his dick tense under the wide angle, pulsing in my mouth nearly as hard as if he was coming straight into my throat.

I managed a shallow breath of air through my nose, then felt like I was about to choke. He must have noticed it in my eyes because he pulled back and let me take a few breaths.

"Was that...okay?" he asked, nearly as breathless as I was. His hand released my hair.

"Fucking perfect," I said and gulped on air. "Do that again."

The fearful look in his eyes disappeared and was replaced by a mischievous grin. "Hell yeah." And he didn't hesitate.

I took a deep breath of air as I opened my mouth as far as I could. His thick cock pushed into me freely this time and I grabbed his ass to make sure he didn't pull back.

I kept my gaze on his handsome face. I reveled in observing his expression change from ecstasy to slight worry, mixed with a painful pressure that was bound to be soaring through his cock.

"Oh, fuck," he murmured a moment before a coughing reflex made my body shudder and my head pull back.

I coughed again and wiped my wet chin with the back of my hand. Probably ridiculous to look at, I shot Gabriel a wet grin as I licked my lips. But in return, his eyes turned wide and heart-shaped and he bent down, pressing an open-mouthed kiss on my lips. He couldn't care less about the mess I'd made and such devotion made my heart soar and my dick tingle and itch.

Gabriel hooked his hands under my arms and lifted me, adding extra pressure on my tightly packed cock. "Take that off," he murmured over my lips.

I kicked my shoes off without breaking away from Gabriel's heated body and scorching kisses. My feet shuffled around and freed themselves off my black pants as Gabriel's hands caressed my arms, neck, and back. He hooked his thumbs inside my underwear and slid the edge down my firm ass, dragging along the front too. My cock was about to explode from the quickly increasing pressure and I sucked the air through my teeth, pushed Gabriel a few inches away, and pulled my boxer-briefs over my upright dick.

Gabriel wasted no time. As soon as my boxer-briefs dropped around my ankles and I lifted a foot to step out of them, his hand closed around my length and gave a long, gentle stroke.

"Get on the sofa," he said, smacking kisses against my lips and chin, gripping my cock harder, and running his other hand up and down the side of my torso.

He let go of me as soon as I smiled and murmured my agreement. Today, I was to be the obedient one, and I couldn't be happier.

I let my hips swing seductively as I walked away from him. A glance over my shoulder found Gabriel's eyes locked onto my lower back and ass. He virtually drooled after me and I felt like the most wanted guy in the world. Never before had I received such adoration in a single glance. Here was a guy who loved all of me and wasn't ashamed of it.

"Kneel," he said in his huskiest, lowest voice.

My heart flickered. Once we were back at Highgate, I would play all his video games because he earned it two times over with this one word.

I bit my lip to suppress an excited smile and let my left knee sink into the sofa, followed by my right. I knelt in the middle and bent forward, folding my arms at the edge and resting my head on them.

Gabriel knelt behind me, gently placing his hands on my hips. His cock nestled between my cheeks and he pulled my body back slowly, sliding his length up until I felt his balls press against my hole. He did it again and again, letting out deep sighs of pleasure, digging his fingers into my hips harder and firmer.

Abruptly, he pushed me forward and crawled a little back, placed his hands on my cheeks, and pulled them apart. His hot breath on my hole made the cabin spin around me. The subdued lamplight seemed somehow dimmer now and I closed my eyes to surrender myself to the sensations as much as I could.

The hot, wet tip of his tongue grazed my skin and I sucked in a long breath of air between my clenched jaws.

A whimper burst out of me without a warning when Gabriel's gentle touch turned fiery and raw. He pushed his open lips hard against my body, his tongue nearly sliding into me. Making me slick with his spit, Gabriel sealed his lips around my hole and did something that I'd never felt before, something that made my cock pulse and leak with precum instantly. He pulled his tongue back and sucked my hole lightly. He kissed it, licked it, sucked it; again and again. Sweat broke out over my back and brow and I gripped the edge of the sofa, grinding my teeth in need to bite something soft. His ear would do nicely were he not so busy edging me closer to my orgasm.

"Fuck, fuck, fuck," I moaned. "Gabriel..."

He didn't stop. In fact, he pressed on harder and faster, pushing his tongue against my hole, squeezing my cheeks, and sucking every so often. His right hand slid down my ass and between my legs where it cupped my tightening balls and found my cock. I swear, the fucker chuckled when he felt my slick tip.

He gave a few lazy strokes just to fan the fire burning in the oven that was my heart. He then pulled his hand back and pressed his index finger against my hole, just next to the tip of his tongue, and probed me without pushing it in. He applied enough pressure that all of me tensed and he did it a few times. Finally, when my muscles relaxed by the sheer force of my will, his finger dipped inside of me, making my eyes roll back in my skull and a shuddering moan leave me from the top of my chest.

Each quickening thrust of his finger and jerky pull back sent waves upon waves of shivers along my spine. Each move he made sent my dick into a pulsing frenzy, pushing precum out of me like it was my sole purpose in life. He was merciless with his moves, twisting his hand at his wrist simultaneously as he penetrated me. His second finger, on a mission to stretch me hard, joined the first. He knew what he was doing, I could tell. He'd been paying attention when he was on the receiving end of this.

Gabriel shoved his two fingers into my body, turned his hand gently left and right, and touched my P-spot, making me cry out with pleasure.

The fucker chuckled in his lowest voice yet.

Pleased with yourself? I meant to ask, but forgot my train of thought momentarily. He pushed his fingers all the way to his knuckles and held them inside as I breathed in tiny bubbles of air.

"Stop teasing me, Gabriel," I pleaded submissively. "I'm going to die."

"No, you're not," he said softly and somehow wiggled his two fingers while all the way inside of me. It sent a tickling bolt through my stomach and groin. I couldn't resist it. The only way to scratch the itch was to grip my cock and stroke it hard for a few good moments.

I moaned into my folded left arm, mouth open all the way. Then, as Gabriel repeated the same move, my teeth sank into my forearm hard and fast. Pain spread along my arm and I let go, leaving the teeth marks on myself.

"Fuck me, please," I grunted, desperate to have him inside of me. I needed him like I needed air and water and sunshine.

His other hand slapped my left cheek as his fingers slipped out of me.

The moment they were out, my hole pulsed rapidly, hungry for more of his body. The lack of his fingers would soon be replaced.

Gabriel got to his feet, emptied his backpack messily around the cabin, and picked up his condoms and lube. He was ready in no time, pouring extra lube into his hand, then massaging my hole gently. He allowed one finger in, briefly, just to tease me extra hard and prepare me for his cock.

But I was so fucking ready by now. I'd been waiting for this for longer than I dared admit. I'd been dreaming about it since I knew how to dream about sex. Finally, he was going to fuck me just like I wanted.

Gabriel picked up his underwear and wiped his hand dry with them, then knelt behind me. "Ready?" he asked.

"Don't waste time asking," I hissed into my folded arm and arched my back a little, raising my ass in the process.

He chuckled softly and I loved him for it. Here was a guy who wasn't ashamed to laugh when he felt like laughing. Even if it was while I wiggled my bare ass for him to take and use.

Gabriel pressed the tip of his cock against my hole and I felt him holding his breath. Hell, I was holding it too. I forced my hole to relax, to take him, but he wasn't so sure anymore. He grunted as he jerked his hips forward and pulled back immediately when I let out a tiny, thin moan.

"Do that again," I said and readied myself. The first one was never the easiest, but what followed was worth every second of potential discomfort. Luckily for us both, I was as brave and horny as Gabriel had always been.

He steadied himself and pressed his dick against me again, but this time, I moved my hand back and touched his hip to keep him still.

Taking a deep breath of air, I pushed back and forced myself down the length of his cock. As he broke into me and as my body accepted him, the breath of air that left my lips was a mixture of a growl and a moan combined.

One of his hands smacked my right shoulder, then the other one did the left. He gripped me hard and grunted as he finished what I started. He jerked his hips forward, thrusting into me with all his muscled might, before pulling back a little, and shoving himself in again, deeper than before.

Mere heartbeats later, Gabriel was catching a quick pace of back and forth, pushing meek whimpers out of my body with each thrust of his hips. The hold on my shoulders soon turned to a pull as he leaned us both back, and I heard myself begging him to go harder and faster and dirtier. "Fuck me any way you want," I was hissing as my fists pushed into the sofa and my head rose high.

Gabriel's hands slid along my shoulders and wrapped around my neck. He held me fast and pulled me back, smashing his body against minc. His grip loosened and his fingers moved along my face as hunger awoke in me.

My mouth dropped open as I panted. My tongue slid out and I moved my head around, trying to get his finger inside my mouth. How he figured out what I was trying to do, I didn't know, but he let two fingers of his right hand slip into my mouth, hooking me like a fish. His left hand did the same, holding my mouth open as I took hungry bites like they were nothing. He stretched my mouth hard as I growled and pushed my ass against him. Our bodies grinding ruthlessly, I bit him harder, only to get a tough jerk of his hands up, lifting my head.

His left hand moved away and held a fistful of hair on the back of my head. Slowly, carefully, he was pulling my hair and lifting me up. My fists hovered, no longer sinking into the sofa, as I rose. Ultimately, I knelt upright and Gabriel wrapped both his arms tightly around my torso, trapped my arms in his steely grip, and rammed me harder. My balls tightened as he relentlessly pushed himself in, hitting my prostate, making my dick leap with excitement.

Breaths stuck in my throat and I choked up as my abs tensed. Every shred of me pulsed and glowed and bloomed. My hole flexed around the base of Gabriel's cock as each thrust of his hips sent my cum shooting out of my upright length. I whimpered and wiggled my right arm to take hold of my cock, gripping it for dear life and jerking it until the very last drop was out, and then some.

My shattering orgasm vibrated through my body as Gabriel took my right hand into his and brought it to his face over my right shoulder. He licked the drops of my wetness off my slender fingers and groaned hard, emptying himself into the condom, pushing his cock balls-deep into me and holding it there as it throbbed and stilled.

"Fuck," I whispered. "That was... Fuck..."

"I know," he panted. "You're so..."

Neither could string more than two words together. His grip on me loosened and I slid off his length, then dropped onto the stained sofa, still dazed.

Gabriel slipped his condom off and lay on top of me with all his weight. It was as though he read my mind and knew exactly what to do. He held me in his arms and pressed down on me in the sweetest, smothering cuddle I'd ever received.

This I could do for the rest of my life.

Epilogue

—ℓℓ—

"It's cold," London said.

His fake sulking face had only grown more beautiful with each new day. "London, it's Christmas."

He wrinkled his nose. "There was nothing wrong with having a Caribbean Christmas. That's all I'm saying." He scratched his chest over a knitted wool sweater with Rudolph across his entire torso. "Ugh." He fake shuddered.

"It's called variety, my love," I said with the patience of a god. I loved his outbursts almost as much as I loved holding him in bed every night, looking forward to waking up next to him.

"It's called 'my balls are freezing' and it's your loss as much as mine," he said, but a corner of his lips cocked up and shattered his sarcastic face with its fiery warmth.

"I do like your balls," I said with all the seriousness of a ball scholar. I picked up a poker and stirred the logs in the fireplace as the colorful Christmas lights danced around the room.

The scent of chocolate fudge filled the small cabin and ensured there was no frost around my heart. Every turn of the lights and every cinnamon spiced scent made me feel fuzzier.

"I never should have mentioned we had this place," London said and twisted on the big, old sofa. "I knew you'd go mad about it."

I snorted. "That's why you mentioned it, babe."

"True." His gaze followed me as I crossed the small cabin and began mixing low-alcohol cocktails. "Are you happy, though?"

"Do you need to ask?" My grin stretched beyond human capacities. I worried that it would get stuck on my face and that I would return to Highgate permanently smiling. That would be a terrible look for an assistant professor.

London dog-eared a page in one of his gooey romance novels, then closed the book and placed it on the small coffee table between the sofa and the fireplace. "Thanks for fueling that fire," he said as he stood up and pulled the knitted sweater over his head. It lifted the tight T-shirt he wore underneath with it and I stopped what I was doing just to get a glance of his sculpted muscles. That never got old. If he walked around naked, every minute of every hour, never to hide his natural beauty, I would still want more. I would still take a moment to gaze and admire him. And I would still wonder if any of this was real or if I was suffering from a concussion. Was he really with me? How in the hell did I get here? And he would grin shortly, let his eyebrows drop flat, and roll his eyes at all my fuzzy softness and doe-eyed adoration.

"I will admit," he went on as he fixed his T-shirt and tugged his gray sweatpants higher over his firm, curvy ass. It was the finest image in the world; London wearing sweatpants. "We needed this break." He walked across the cabin to the kitchen island and folded his arms on its marble top. "You especially, mister."

I smiled at that. It was far from something I was willing to admit, but the last couple of years pushed me close to burning out. It had all been for a good reason and the reason was this. I'd graduated in time to start my Master's without taking a break, then speed-graduated from there so I could take up the assistant professor job as soon as one opened. I'd been tapped by my mentor for it the moment there was an opening. And now, I was working all my waking hours, getting ready to start my PhD next fall.

"You're making it sound like I had a bad time," I scolded.

"Not with me," he said with an air of satisfaction. "God, no. I'm all the fun. I'm the best. But you know, in the real world." He laughed.

"You *are* the best," I said.

He snorted. "I know. I just said that."

He still didn't believe it. But he was. Had I been on my own, not a lot would have happened. Definitely not enough for a story. But London had stood with me every step of the way, helped me at every turn, and showered me with the kind of love I regret not showing him for that entire decade of his unrequited love from afar. Making up for that was my mission in life. Everything else was just details.

He'd been with me when Dad made his first contact with me after a year and a half of silence. He'd been with me when that first conversation went south. And he'd been there for every conversation that followed.

We weren't in the clear, yet, Dad and I. But there was still hope. If I found it in my heart to be a little more forgiving and if he found it in his to be a little open, perhaps we might see eye to eye. Perhaps. Rome wasn't built in a day. But one thing is for sure, building Rome would have been easier if all the kings, consuls, and emperors had London by their side to roll his eyes sarcastically and go out of his way to make them laugh at least once a day.

The nearing engine purr wrinkled London's brow. "Are we expecting someone?"

My heart jumped up and down in my chest, trashing and tittering with excitement. "Stay there. I have a surprise."

"Oh my God, a threesome? You *do* listen," he said with bubbling joy.

I laughed out loud. "Better."

"Better than three?" He shook his head at himself. We'd discussed threesomes once in fact, and London was decisively against the idea, to my relief. He was a possessive one; but then again, so was I. *I'm not sharing you with anyone.*

The car that had reached us up in the picturesque, snowy Vermont hills where London's family owned this cabin, stopped in the driveway. I threw on my coat and scarf, then walked outside to greet the guy I'd been talking to for days. We'd done all the paperwork virtually, which had been a challenge with London always present. I'd done it from my modest office at Highgate in the end.

The snow outside was glowing from the front deck lights as well as the car's headlights. It snowed very little now, with an odd snowflake here and there, but the heaps of snow on each side of the driveway were a testament to the power of the elements and our backs. We'd been shoveling for half a day.

The young man who'd arrived this evening was a scrawny thing with a bright, warm smile and big, blue eyes. He wore a red beanie and had his scarf tucked messily into his thick winter jacket. "How are ya?" he asked as he pushed out a hand for a shake.

"Glad to see you got here safely," I said.

"I'm used to driving in this weather," he said with a casual shrug. "And here's the little guy." He headed to the passenger door and looked at me before opening it. "Don't worry. The box has air holes and I only just closed it."

I chuckled. I hadn't worried until he told me not to. Now, I wasn't so sure. But he smiled more and I decided I could trust him. He was, after all, a professional.

"Is this his new home?" the guy asked, gesturing with his head at the orange glowing cabin behind me.

"No, no. We're just staying here for a few days. He'll be heading to Santa Barbara with us." My heart skipped another beat. I didn't know what excited me more; the idea of meeting the little fellow or seeing the look on London's face.

"I'll get you a travel crate if you need one," the guy said.

"Sure thing. The day after tomorrow is good," I said.

"Totally," he agreed.

Though I expected we wouldn't need a crate. I expected London to never let go of his best-friend-to-be. Since we'd moved into our new house after London graduated — with the massive help from his family as a way of celebrating London's graduation, to be honest — we lacked something to spice up our lives.

"Well, here goes," the guy said and opened the passenger door. The box was rather large and had red and gold wrapping paper glued to all its outside parts. It was dotted with plenty of big holes at the top and on the sides.

I took the box carefully, hearing nothing from inside of it. I thanked the guy and confirmed the order for the crate, then hurried back to the cabin to protect London's present from the cold.

Just as I neared the door, it flew open, and London stared at me with suspicion. "What did you do?"

I laughed and walked inside, then carefully placed the box on the floor as the engine purr faded away and London closed the door.

"Open it," I said.

London fought his smile to the last moment. He really tried suppressing it, but the smile prevailed. "I'm scared," he said.

"There's nothing to be scared about," I promised.

He slowly knelt next to the box and the first scraping sound came from it. Nervous laughter burst out of London as he wiggled his fingers above the box. "Oh, what did you do, Gabriel?" But this time, it was rhetorical, and he was reaching for the top of the box, then lifted it.

His jaw hit the floor at once, eyes shining with happy tears that pooled there instantly. A long, heart-melting 'aw' left his pretty, red lips as he let the lid of the box drop on the floor.

Just then, a clumsy, high-pitched, unpracticed 'woof' came from the box as a greeting and my heart just about exploded like fireworks against a midnight sky. The long, dark gray and white tail began to wag as London reached inside the box to lift his puppy out of the clean rags he'd traveled on.

"A Siberian Husky," London said in a way one might recite a poem.

"His name is Spirit," I said as I knelt on the other side of the box to watch a boy and a dog begin a bond that would last their lifetimes.

London's cheeks became wet when those big, happy tears rolled down and he threw his head to his shoulder to wipe them off, but couldn't reach it while scratching the gray and white fur. So I reached with my hand and brushed my thumb over his cheeks. Even I was about to cry, warmth soaring through me, melting every bit of my soul.

"Just when I thought you couldn't make me any happier," he whispered in a choked up voice.

He looked into my eyes with those big, brown chestnuts of his twinkling and shook his head as though to say he couldn't believe it.

"I told you a million times we were a family," I said. "And frankly, three years in, it's time to expand our family." And, after a moment, I added, "Now, we can be just the way you've imagined us all those years ago." I still had his sketchbook.

"Did you hear that, Spirit?" London asked the pup who was excitedly moving left and right, sniffing my soulmate's knees and hands, licking him fervently. "You've got one of the best dads in the world, you know?" he told the puppy. "And I love him very, very much," he added in a whisper.

And when he looked at me again, my heart was fuller than I had ever thought possible.

The End

Want more? Be sure to visit haydenhallwrites.com and subscribe to receive all my free stories, monthly magazine, and alerts when my future books come out. Your membership is the most valuable resource for an independent author like me and I greatly appreciate it.

Frat Brats of Santa Barbara

A Quick Note

If you enjoyed this book, please leave an honest review on Amazon (also Goodreads and Bookbub, if you use them). Reader reviews are the single most important factor of any author's success, and they're ten times as important for the independent authors like me. They help others decide whether to read the book or not. Drop a line and help others!

The story of The Fuckboys continues in *The Bitter Rivals Fiasco*. If you like enemies to lovers romances, be ready for it.

Also, grab Alex and Franklyn's story, *The Last Summer Vacation*. The perks include access to all my exclusive content, a free monthly magazine, and discount alerts. You can join my mailing list by visiting www.haydenhallwrites.com

And finally, if you're looking for something else to read in the meantime, you should check out *The Two Stars Collision*. It's a fake dating story with a ton of *Star Wars* references, opposites attract trope, and a grand finale to blow your mind. It's a complete standalone in my *College Boys* series.

Acknowledgments

Thank you, dear reader, for giving *The Wrong Twin Dilemma* a chance. All I can say is that I truly hope, in my heart of hearts, that you have enjoyed it. If a book of mine makes you smile, even once, I take that as a victory. This one made me smile many times while I was writing it.

This is the third *Frat Brats of Santa Barbara* book. It feels like it was only yesterday when I sat down to write the opening line of *The Fake Boyfriends Debacle*. Time flies like mad. But this entire series has been a joy to write and I'm looking forward to many, many more months playing in this sandbox of mine.

However, playing in the sandbox is one thing, but publishing a finished book is quite another. It would be impossible without so many people who are directly and indirectly involved in the creation of each of these stories.

My most sincere gratitude to Sabrina for her patience, keen eye, and laugh-out-loud comments throughout the manuscripts, which I find each new morning of writing. You've done it again! You've made me spit my black coffee over my laptop more than I care to admit.

Huge thank you to Xander for sticking with me through the writing process. It somehow seems that, whenever I start a new book, I forget everything I thought I had learned. Xander is always there to remind me that banging my head against the wall is very much my usual writing routine.

And thank you, the reader, for picking up any one of my books, and going, "I think I'll stick around for this one." Because of you, everything seems possible.

Love,
Hayden Hall

Made in the USA
Coppell, TX
02 July 2022

79498719R00150